Francis Seymour Haden

The Life and Genius of Rembrandt

The most celebrated of Rembrandt's etchings : thirty photographs taken from the

collections in the British Museum, and in the possession of Mr. Seymour Haden

Francis Seymour Haden

The Life and Genius of Rembrandt
The most celebrated of Rembrandt's etchings : thirty photographs taken from the collections in the British Museum, and in the possession of Mr. Seymour Haden

ISBN/EAN: 9783337384401

Printed in Europe, USA, Canada, Australia, Japan

Cover: Foto ©Raphael Reischuk / pixelio.de

More available books at **www.hansebooks.com**

THE LIFE AND GENIUS OF REMBRANDT.

THE MOST CELEBRATED OF

REMBRANDT'S ETCHINGS

THIRTY PHOTOGRAPHS TAKEN FROM THE COLLECTIONS IN THE

BRITISH MUSEUM, AND IN THE POSSESSION

OF MR. SEYMOUR HADEN.

WITH DESCRIPTIONS: AND A DISCOURSE ON THE LIFE AND GENIUS OF REMBRANDT,

BY DR. SCHELTEMA, OF AMSTERDAM.

EDITED BY JOSEPH CUNDALL.

LONDON:

BELL AND DALDY, 186, FLEET STREET,

CAMBRIDGE: DEIGHTON, BELL, AND CO.

1867.

PREFACE.

IT is not to the credit of the literary men of Holland, that, for nearly a century and a half, they allowed the fame of one of their most celebrated countrymen to lie under a heavy cloud, when it is now evident that it might have been easily dispelled. Nearly all that has hitherto passed as the Life of Rembrandt Van Rhyn emanated from the pen of Arnold Houbraken, an engraver, who published, at Amsterdam, in the year 1718, a series of portraits of distinguished Dutch painters, and with them gave some slight account of their lives. Nearly every assertion which he made in his Memoir of Rembrandt, which was written within fifty years of that artist's death, has been proved to be incorrect. Rembrandt was not born in a mill on the Rhine,—as Houbraken asserts,—but in the town of Leyden, where his father lived in good circumstances, and was part proprietor of the mill he worked. He did not marry a peasant girl of Ransdorp, but the daughter of a Doctor of Laws, who was one of the chief magistrates of the town of Leeuwarden, in Friesland, and who gave his daughter a rich dowry. He

b

could not have been the associate of low-bred fellows, or the wretch
that Houbraken makes him, or he would not have been on terms of
friendship with Professor Tulp, one of the most celebrated men in
Amsterdam of his day; nor with Tulp's wealthy son-in-law, the
Burgomaster Six; nor with Uytenbogaert, the Chaplain to the
Prince of Orange and the friend of Arminius; nor with the other
Uytenbogaert, the banker; nor with the celebrated preacher Jan
Cornelius Silvius, who was related to him by marriage; nor with the
poet Decker, who wrote poems in his praise. That he was an
uneducated man is also proved to be an error, for his letters to
Constantine Huygens, the Secretary of Prince Frederic Henri, which
are still preserved, prove him to have been, at all events, fairly
educated, and are evidently the productions of an unassuming
gentleman.

Nor could Rembrandt have been miserly or avaricious, for he
spent money freely, perhaps too freely, in the purchase of works
of art, with which his house was filled; and he did not die in
possession of riches, for, alas! it is too well proved that his last
days were spent in comparative poverty.

What reason Houbraken had for vilifying his illustrious countryman we shall probably never discover,—though it is a matter
worth much investigation. Rembrandt has now found a champion
who is in every way worthy of the task he has undertaken;
a learned archivist of Amsterdam has searched every public docu-
ment which is likely to throw light on the name of Rembrandt,

and when the citizens of Amsterdam (in rivalry of their brethren at Antwerp, who not long since set up a statue to Rubens), determined to raise a statue in honour of their greatest painter, Dr. Scheltema delivered a Discourse which can never be forgotten, inasmuch as it, for the first time, gave the result of his investigations, and proved that the aspersions on the character of Rembrandt which Houbraken originated, were nothing better than dishonest fables.

As an artist, Rembrandt has never been fully appreciated in England, except by connoisseurs who have had access to his best works. His own countrymen have always preserved his finest paintings, which may still be seen in the galleries of Amsterdam and the Hague, and his world-renowned etchings arc far too expensive to be in the possession of any but wealthy amateurs. It is through the liberality of the Trustees of the British Museum and Mr. Seymour Haden that we are enabled to offer excellent transcripts of the most celebrated of these etchings ; and that the names of the Burgomaster Six, Ephraim Bonus, Cornelius Silvius, and the other worthy citizens of Amsterdam whom Rembrandt has immortalized, will now be made familiar where they have been hitherto but little known.

All the photographs have been taken from rare and choice proofs, such as are very seldom to be met with, and the greatest possible care has been taken in their production. The impressions of "The Angel appearing to the Shepherds," "The Resurrection of Lazarus," "Christ Healing the Sick," (the hundred guilder piece), "The Ecce Homo," and "The Death of the Virgin," as well as many others, are from etchings in the finest state, which are amongst the richest treasures of the British Museum, and not only our thanks, but the thanks of all lovers of art, are due to the Trustees for their generosity in allowing these copies to be made.

The works to which we are chiefly indebted for the information contained in the following pages are Dr. Scheltema's *Rembrand, Discours sur sa Vie et son Génie,* annotée par W. Bürger, and Bartsch's *Catalogue raisonné de toutes les Estampes qui forment l'œuvre de Rembrandt.* We have also availed ourselves of the researches of M. Charles Blanc, who has written a most valuable book upon the works of Rembrandt, and published in an expensive form photographs of nearly all his important etchings.

CONTENTS.

PHOTOGRAPHS OF THE ETCHINGS.

(*Photographed by Cundall and Fleming.*)

DISCOURSE ON

THE LIFE AND GENIUS OF REMBRANDT.

ON

THE LIFE AND GENIUS OF REMBRANDT.

A DISCOURSE DELIVERED AT AMSTERDAM IN MAY, 1852,

BY DR. SCHELTEMA.[1]

UR countrymen have sometimes been accused of ingratitude, or at least of indifference to the memory of our great men. Although I cannot, in general, admit the grounds of this reproach, I am, nevertheless, obliged to acknowledge that the merits of some of our most eminent countrymen have had but little light thrown upon them by the pen of our historians, and that we have not, until the present time, taken sufficient pains to transmit their names to posterity, with the honours which are their due.[1]

Only a few amongst them, such as Huig de Groot (Hugo Grotius) and Michael de Ruyter, have obtained the distinction of having had their biographies carefully and completely written. Of several others, whose names are cited even by foreigners with admiration, we know next to nothing with certainty, and but little has been written about them. It is astonishing that amongst these last we must place the name of the unique Rembrandt Van Ryn, the man who is at the head of the ancient school of Dutch painting, and who occupies

---

[1] This Discourse is translated from "REMBRANDT, DISCOURS SUR SA VIE ET SON GÉNIE," par Le DOCTEUR SCHELTEMA, Chevalier de la Couronne de Chêne; Annotée par W. BÜRGER, Paris, 1866.—ED.

[2] The Society *Arti et Amicitiæ*, to whom M. Scheltema delivered this discourse, is composed of all the eminent artists and distinguished amateurs of Holland.

the same place of honour as that assigned to Rubens in the Flemish School of the seventeenth century. Doubtless we know Rembrandt by the admirable productions of his paint-brush and his graver; we see in his works how, by means of a striking application of light and shade, he produced the most marvellous effects; we know that he possessed, in a great degree, the art of animating, as it were, his paper or his canvas by the truthfulness of his representations; but as to the character, or the life of this admirable artist, there are only a very few accounts, and these, for the most part, unjust or incorrect, which have been handed down to us.

This perhaps was one of the motives which, a few years ago, decided the Dutch Society of Arts and Sciences to offer to competition an Eulogium on Rembrandt.

The reply sent by the learned Immerzeel obtained the silver medal.[1] This discourse, considered as an Eulogium—and that was what the Society demanded—has merits which must be acknowledged; but has the writer fulfilled the promise made in the preface, of eliminating from his work all that had been falsely advanced or manifestly invented concerning the life of Rembrandt, and of placing our painter in the clear light of truth? I think not. Scarcely anything is to be met with in this discourse which is not to be found in preceding authors, or which can pass either as new or unknown, except one important particular concerning a sad circumstance in the life of the artist which is communicated to us for the first time by Immerzeel. Moreover, the same errors, the same inaccuracies reappear in his work which, from the time of Houbraken, to whom they seem to owe their birth, up to the present, have been regularly transmitted from one writer to another, occasionally with the addition of new fictions.

To-morrow our country will accord to its Rembrandt the honour which a few years ago was bestowed upon Rubens in the town of Antwerp. The statue raised to Rembrandt in one of our principal places will be solemnly

---

[1] In the year 1839.

uncovered,[1] and the Amstel will no longer have to envy the prerogative of the Scheldt.

It seemed to me, that, especially at this moment, there was an absolute necessity that new efforts should be made to throw light on the life of Rembrandt. I imagined that, for more than one reason, I might be expected to undertake this task—that it was, in fact, a duty prescribed to me by my country.

Obedient to this voice, I have entered upon this study, the fruits of which I now modestly offer.

It must not, however, be expected of me that, speaking on this occasion of Rembrandt, I should dare to place myself in the position of judge or censor of his works, nor that I should endeavour to point out or explain all the originality and beauty which distinguish his productions.

The famous Carthaginian general, Hannibal—exiled from his country— having retired to the Court of Antiochus the Great, at Ephesus, was invited to hear a discourse by the peripatetic philosopher, Phormion. The orator spoke before him of the duties of a general and of the various parts of the military art. After the close of the discourse, those who were present, and who had listened with much pleasure, asked the Carthaginian what he thought of the philosopher. Hannibal made this brief but sensible reply, " I have seen many fools in the course of my life, but never so great a fool as Phormion." " Assuredly he was not wrong," remarks Cicero, with regard to this anecdote, which he has related in his book *De Ora-tore*. What could be more foolish or more impudent than to pretend, without ever having seen either camp or enemy, and without having had any public employment, to give lessons in the military art to Hannibal, who, for so many years, disputed the empire of the world with the Romans, the conquerors of all nations ?

[1] The Statue of Rembrandt, by L. Royer, in the Butter-market in Amsterdam, was uncovered, with great ceremony, in the presence of the king, William III, on the 27th of May, 1852.—ED.

I should not deserve a more favourable judgment if I undertook to give lessons in painting, or endeavoured to unveil all the riches of Rembrandt's brilliant genius before auditors more competent than myself to appreciate that genius ; for I am happy to see present amongst us men who, whatever may be the decadence of our country in arts and sciences, still maintain worthily the ancient glory of the Dutch School.

At first, I intended to have given a concise but exact account of the life of Rembrandt, and afterwards to have communicated some observations on his personal qualities and character.   It seems to me, however, that in thus limiting my discourse I should be tracing an image without force or colour, since, after all, the idea we form of a person is inseparably connected with the idea of his profession.   So, after having set forth before you his biography and his personal qualities, I shall throw a rapid *coup d'œil* on his merit as an artist. The opinion that I shall express about his works is partly formed from my own artistic feeling, but it is gained in a greater degree from the knowledge of experienced men.

If I depart from the opinion of preceding writers on some of the principal points in the life of Rembrandt, I must not be accused of the desire of announcing something new, nor of the still more futile desire of correcting and criticising others.   My facts are drawn from authentic sources ; they rest upon a solid foundation, as I hope to make my countrymen acknowledge by the publication of this work, and the honourable secretary of the society *Arti et Amicitiæ* has willingly promised me his assistance in making known to foreigners the truth on this subject.[1]

According to general opinion, Rembrandt Hermanszoon Van Ryn[2] was born in 1606.   I think, however, that I shall be able to prove that he did not

---

[1] M. Alexander Oltmans was not able to keep his promise, for he died on the 10th of April, 1853. But in 1859, in the *Revue universelle des Arts*, published in Paris and Brussels, there appeared a translation of my work, reviewed and annotated by W. Bürger.

[2] Rembrandt, the son of Herman of the Rhine.

come into the world until two years after that date, viz. in 1608.[1] I also think that the place of his birth has been wrongly indicated. A mill, situated near the Rhine, between the villages of Leiderdorp and Koudekerk, has been assigned as the locality. It appears to me, however, very probable that Rembrandt was born in Leyden. It is, at all events, certain that his grandparents Gerrit Roelofszoon Van Ryn and Lijsbeth Hermansdochter, as well as his parents Herman Gerritszoon Van Ryn and Neeltje Willemsdochter von Zuidbroek[2] always lived[3] in Leyden, in a house situated in the Weddesteeg near the Wittepoort (the White Gate). They lived in a malt-mill, of which they were half owners.

The parents of Rembrandt were bourgeois in easy circumstances, who, at their death, left a pretty considerable property, comprising, besides other estates, a pleasure-garden at Zoeterwoude. But the succession to this property did not fall on Rembrandt alone as one might have concluded it would, since he has always been represented as the only child of his parents. He had, however, six brothers and sisters, all mentioned by name in the public register of the town of Leyden. Of the seven children, of whom Rembrandt was the sixth, there were, besides himself, three who were alive in 1640, in which year the mother died (the father having died some years before), and with whom he shared the family inheritance. A writer who is worthy of credit[4] relates that Rembrandt's parents sent him to school in Leyden, with the intention of having him afterwards taught Latin, in order that he might enter the University of Leyden and render himself capable of holding some office in the town or state.

Rembrandt then, as well as Rubens, was in the first instance destined to

---

[1] Rembrandt, in his marriage registry (on the 10th June, 1634) and in the *Pinbock* (the public registry) of the city of Amsterdam, declares himself to be twenty-six years of age.

[2] His grandparents were Gerrit, the son of Roelof of the Rhine, and Elizabeth, the daughter of Herman; and his parents, Herman, the son of Gerrit of the Rhine, and Cornelia, the daughter of William of the village of Zuidbroek.—ED.

[3] From the year 1590 to 1646.—*M. R. Elsevier.*

[4] Orlers, *Description of Leyden*.

the study of jurisprudence. But this vocation did not at all accord with the taste and inclination of the young boy, who, even thus early in life, felt stirring in his breast a decided love for drawing and painting. His parents, giving in to this desire, had him taught the principles of these arts by Jakob Isaakszoon van Swanenburg, a painter but little known. He remained with this master about three years, and made such progress during that period that it might have been predicted, from the imperfect sketches of the young man, that his talent, in its development, would one day produce something great.

Rembrandt was afterwards placed by his father at Amsterdam, under Pieter Lastman, whom Vondel—certainly by a poetic figure—has styled the Apelles of his age. He only remained six months in Lastman's school, and pursued his studies under the direction of Jakob Pinas, a painter of Haarlem. He only stopped a short time with this master, and soon returned to the paternal abode in Leyden. Here he continued to exercise himself in the use of the graver and paintbrush, and soon acquired such a reputation as a painter that he was frequently sent for to take portraits in Amsterdam. This induced him to establish himself in that town about the year 1630.

Rembrandt lived in several different places in Amsterdam. The first of his dwellings that can be determined upon with certainty is that in Sint Antonie Breestraat (Great St. Anthony Street), where he lived in 1634. Five years later, we find him dwelling on the Binnen Amstel (Inner Amstel). It appears, however, that he did not remain there long, and that he returned to Sint Antonie Breestraat, where he bought a large house situated in that part of the street now named Joden Breestraat (Great Jew's Street), the second house after the lock of St. Antonie on the south side. He spent a great part of the remainder of his life in this dwelling, where he executed the greater number of his *chefs-d'œuvre*, without leaving the town of Amsterdam. The last place he lived in was a house at the end of the Rozengracht (Canal of Roses), opposite the ancient Doolhof (Labyrinth).

In 1634 Rembrandt married Saskia Uilenburg. The marriage was celebrated on the 22nd of June of this year, in Friesland, in the parish of St. Anne, where Saskia was living with her sister Hiskia, who was married to Gerrit van Loo, Secretary of the bailiwick of Bildt (de Grietenij het Bildt). The biographers of Rembrandt have wrongly stated his wife to have been a little peasant girl of Ransdorp in Waterland. Far from being descended from a race of peasants, she was, on the contrary, the issue of a very distinguished and very respectable Friesland family. Saskia was the daughter of Rombertus Uilenburg, a burgher-master and magistrate[1] of the town of Leeuwarden, and who afterwards occupied, for several years, the dignified position of Counsellor of the Court of Friesland, which he filled with distinction. He had. eight children, of whom Saskia, the fourth of the daughters, appears to have been the seventh. It is related, as a remarkable circumstance in the life of this Rombertus Uilenburg, that he happened to be at Delft as a delegate from the Friesland towns, on the 10th July, 1584, the day on which William I. was assassinated, and that he dined with the prince shortly before the perpetration of the crime. About two o'clock William got up from the table, and a few moments after, whilst descending the staircase of the Court, he was treacherously shot by Balthazar Gerards.[2]

Saskia Uilenburg was not only a woman of distinction, but moreover she was rich. A sentence of the Court of Friesland apprises us that she was one day reproached with having, by her luxury and pomp, wasted the inheritance of her parents,—a charge which does not appear to have had any foundation. Saskia and Rembrandt might, without vanity, boast of being richly and superabundantly laden with temporal goods, and it is said, " that they could never sufficiently thank the Almighty for it." Rembrandt had not the happiness

---

[1] Pensionary of Leeuwarden.

[2] M. G. H. M. Delprat has made known this circumstance by publishing (in " Documents to be used for the History of Holland, etc," vol. ii. p. 119) a letter from Uilenburg to the magistrate of Leeuwarden, concerning the reception of William I. at Delft, and his death on the 10th of July, 1584.

M. Gachard, Keeper of the Bourgogne Library at Brussels, has reproduced this letter in his Preface to Vol. VI. of the Correspondence of William the Silent.—W. B.

of possessing his wife for more than eight years. Saskia Uilenburg died in this town[1] in the middle of June, 1642, and was buried on the 19th, in the old church (Oude Kerk). We know that she left Rembrandt a son named Titus, who was brought up by his father in his own profession, but who in no wise distinguished himself as an artist. It is not commonly known, and the fact is of little importance, that another child had been born before Titus, who died young, and was buried in the south church (Zuider Kerk) on the 13th of August, 1638. By her will, Saskia made her son Titus Van Ryn her heir, with the condition that Rembrandt, her husband, until he re-married, (and if he should not re-marry until his death), should have full possession and usufruct of the property that she left, charged with the expense of giving Titus an honourable education and providing suitably for his wants until he attained his majority, or until he married, in which latter case he was to receive from his father a marriage portion or endowment. It was moreover stipulated that if Titus died before his father, and without legitimate descendants, Rembrandt should inherit the whole; and that at his death, or if he contracted a new marriage, one half of the property should remain on his side and the other half should go to Hiskia, the sister of Saskia, on condition of her making some legacies to her own relations.

After the death of Saskia, Rembrandt contracted a new marriage, about which I know nothing certain, except that two children were the result of it.

I have already said that scarcely anything is known of the life of Rembrandt. He did not seek the society of the great, nor did he win credit and consideration by his social relations.

Rubens frequented the palaces of the nobility and the courts of princes; important embassies were confided to him, which spread his glory and his name abroad. Rembrandt lived only for his studies and for the instruction of his pupils, who assembled in great numbers around him. Rubens dwelt alternately in several of the countries of Europe. Italy, Spain, France, and

[1] Amsterdam.

England possessed him in turns for a considerable time; whilst Rembrandt, well known to his fellow-citizens and countrymen, but scarcely famous beyond his own country, passed his life within the walls of his studio.

Three engravings by Rembrandt have led some to imagine that he must have been in Venice. Some writers assert that he lived in England and in Sweden. Both conjectures are entirely erroneous. From the year 1630 until his death he always had his home in Amsterdam, and he seldom appears to have left this town; and even when he did, it was only for a short time,—certainly never to travel abroad. I am ignorant whether Rembrandt was a burgher of Amsterdam. It is very probable that, like Govert Flinck and Ferdinand Bol, and other of his pupils, he enjoyed the burghership.

" Rembrandt," says Houbraken, " must necessarily have amassed a large sum of money, for he lived in a bourgeois style and gained much by his art; yet after his death his estate was not found to be worth very much." This writer, who was very ill-informed upon all that concerns the life of Rembrandt, and who has judged his talent with injustice and partiality, was evidently not aware of a misfortune which befel our artist in 1656; otherwise he would have learnt that Rembrandt's productions, sought after with ever-increasing interest at a later date, were far from bringing him treasure in his lifetime. In the year above-mentioned Rembrandt was declared insolvent, and his property passed to the Desolate Boedelkamor (Court of Insolvents). His house in Sint Antonie Breestraat, his furniture and his linen, his pictures and his drawings,[1]—in one word, all that he possessed,—were sold by a judicial execution. It is true that this misfortune did not stifle his love for art, nor lessen his ardour in work; but it appears that, embittered by the losses he had experienced, he retired into solitude, and from that time forth was so little remarked in the world, that, for a long time, the place and the time of his death remained in complete uncertainty. Some writers have presumed that Rembrandt, after his misfortune, established himself in some town in England;

[1] A very interesting Catalogue of the property which was sold is given in the Appendix.

C

others pretend that he died in Stockholm. Finally, Immerzeel thought to put an end to the discussion by publishing a note of the register of burial in the cemetery of Sint Antonie, according to which Rembrandt was interred there on the 19th of July, 1664.[1]

This statement, the authenticity of which has already been contested, on account of the existence of a picture executed by Rembrandt in 1667,[2] I have found, upon examination, to be incorrect. I have discovered that Rembrandt died in 1669, at Amsterdam, on the Rozengracht. His mortal remains were interred, on the 8th of October of the same year, in the West Church (Wester Kerk) of this town.

But if the accounts which ancient authors have given of Rembrandt's life are incomplete and inexact, we may certainly say the same of those which relate to his character.

We are well acquainted with his outward appearance by means of the number of portraits he has left us of himself, with his features full of vigour and expression, and his eyes sparkling with intelligence and life; but I think we should form a very false idea of his inward qualities if we were to place faith in the strange particulars that have been related concerning his mode of living and acting. Rembrandt has been represented to us as a man of coarse manners, who sought his amusements amongst the lowest classes of the people. He was, it has been said, a man given up to cupidity and avarice, and yet who, at the same time, absurd as this may seem, was not free from the opposite

---

[1] Immerzeel. *Lofrede op Rembrandt* (*Eulogium of Rembrandt*), pp. 47 and 59.

[2] According to Nagler, Rathgeber, and several other writers, there is a picture by him, signed and dated 1669. It is the one numbered 271 in the Darmstadt Museum, "A woman cleaning the head of her child, who is eating an apple; a dog has opened the door with his front paw, and is going out. Signed by name. On canvas."—*Catalogue of the Darmstadt Museum*, 1843. We see that this catalogue, which mentions the signature, does not speak of the curious date. There is a date however, but the last figures are almost illegible. There is no doubt that it is really 1649, and not 1669; and the style of the painting quite confirms this date.

vices of prodigality and dissipation. If there is anything which, in the course of my researches, has awakened in me a feeling of satisfaction, and has augmented my respect for our illustrious countryman, it is the discovery that these calumnious rumours are nothing but falsehoods and fables. I am happy to say that, in spite of the scarceness of documents, there still exist proofs sufficient to upset most completely all these accusations.

It is quite possible that Rembrandt was acquainted with simple bourgeois people of a low class, and even that he sought their society, without there being anything dishonourable to him in so doing.[1] We find the same peculiarity in other great geniuses without its being made a reproach to them. The celebrated Junius, when he composed his *Nomenclator*, or Vocabulary, in eight languages, was not ashamed to hold conversations with workmen and artisans, in order to learn the right names of the instruments and tools used in their professions. And how much useful information might not our painter have acquired from similar conversations, devoted as he was to an art whose practice demands an almost universal knowledge. But that Rembrandt attached himself solely and by preference to the most degraded class of society is what I can emphatically contradict. Our excellent poet, Jeremias de Decker, who is known to us, by his works, as an upright and religious man, called Rembrandt his friend, in a sonnet composed in honour of the painter; and Rembrandt, in his turn, gave him a true proof of sympathy by painting, out of pure affection, the portrait of the poet. This caused Decker to again

---

[1] M. Scheltema's anxiety to justify Rembrandt for having mixed with the lower orders of the people is rather exaggerated; and Gerard Le Nerval. who heard him deliver his Discourse to the Society *Arti et Amicitiæ*, did not fail, in *La Revue des Deux Mondes*, to reproach the learned and honourable archivist of Amsterdam with this excessive piece of prudery. Rembrandt was like all truly great artists; he frequented both the highest and the lowest society, he was acquainted with distinguished men of all sorts in the great city of Amsterdam, with painters, poets, learned men, politicians, and with all people of position of whatever kind: but he also sought for and found *men* amongst the eccentric classes of the Jews' quarter, amongst the labouring or the adventurous population of Amsterdam. It was thence that he took his original, strange, and sometimes savage types. Life, mind, courage, beauty, picturesque forms, are they not to be found everywhere?—W. B.

take up his lyre and express, in some beautiful verses, his gratitude for the distinction accorded him. Rembrandt also enjoyed the friendship and con· fidence of the celebrated Professor Nikolaas Tulp, and of Tulp's son-in-law, Jan Six, of Vromade. Of his friendly relations with the last-named person I have found a decisive proof. There fell into my hands, by chance, an album which had belonged to Six, and which contains two pages of sketches by Rembrandt. Now, if Jan Six, who was a lover of art, had only been a patron, or played the part of a Mæcenas towards Rembrandt, he would certainly not have accorded him a place in his album. And it is of a man like Rembrandt, who could boast of possessing the friendship and esteem of a Decker, a Tulp, and a Six, that people have dared to say, that he sought his pleasure in the society of low and vulgar people. Truly, this reproach does not need a more ample refutation.

Another accusation brought against Rembrandt has a greater appearance of truth. He has been accused of cupidity and avarice; and this seems, at first sight, to have some foundation: but, after impartial examination, it is found to be utterly futile and baseless. For, how can we conclude that he was avaricious from the fact that he once put out his hand to take up a piece of money painted on the ground, or some other place, by one of his pupils? What man, however disinterested, might not have been the dupe of such an artifice? And what shall we say of the odious charge made against him, of having sent his son to sell his prints below their value, under the pretext that they had been stolen? Or of this other story,—That he caused his wife to spread a report of his death, in order that his works might fetch a higher price? What father, in his right senses, would give such an order to his son? What honest husband would exact such a thing from his wife? It is equally incredible that Rembrandt, so easily recognized by his physiognomy and his peculiar costume, should have attended the public auctions, hoping not to be known, in order to run up the price of his own works.

Even his custom of working up the different editions of the same plate has been attributed to a vile avaricious sentiment, although he evidently had but one aim, that of improving and perfecting his proofs. Thus does calumny turn everything to account in order to attain her shameful purposes, transforming good into ill, and representing as blameable that which is worthy of praise.

But enough, perhaps too much, concerning these frivolous anecdotes. Do we, on the other hand, desire a proof of Rembrandt's discretion and disinterestedness? I will quote from three letters written by him to the celebrated Constantijn Hiugens. The Prince Frederik Hendrik had ordered two paintings of Rembrandt for his collection, representing *The Entombment* and *The Resurrection.* When sending these two pictures to Hiugens, the Prince's secretary, Rembrandt wrote, telling him the price at which he estimated them, but he added, " If the Prince thinks this price too high, he is at liberty to give me less, for I refer the matter to his judgment and discretion, and I shall gratefully content myself with the sum he offers." In a second letter in which Rembrandt modestly requests the sum which is due to him for the pictures ordered by the Prince, the price of which had been fixed, not at 2000 florins, as Rembrandt had hoped, but only at 1200 florins, the artist does not show the least irritation at this, nor manifest any discontent at the delay in payment. In a third letter Rembrandt politely offers Hiugens a picture of his own painting, as a mark of his cordial sympathy,—behaviour which does not accord with the nature of an avaricious man.

This accusation of avarice is still more completely refuted by the sad loss of fortune he afterwards experienced. It appears strange, certainly, that he should have got into such difficulties, inhabiting, as he did, his own house, and enjoying the use of the property left by his wife, besides the considerable income he obtained from his paintings, etchings, and lessons. Sandrart estimates that Rembrandt made more than 2500 florins a-year by pupils. Besides this, he executed numerous works. In the principal galleries of Europe we can now reckon about a hundred and fifty of Rembrandt's pictures, without counting those that are to be met with in private collections. No collection of drawings can pretend to be even tolerably complete if it does not contain some production of his pencil. If we consider, moreover, that the number of his etchings amounts to three hundred and seventy-six, the different states of which are almost innumerable, we shall feel amazed at the power of production in a genius who could produce, in the lifetime of a man, so many original and finished works.

The contradiction, which results from the decrease of Rembrandt's fortune and his unexampled assiduity in work, has brought upon him the suspicion of prodigality and dissipation. Nevertheless, we know that he lived in a very simple manner, and that often, whilst at work, his repast consisted only of a bit of bread and cheese, or a red herring. He spent very little either at home or abroad, and was rarely seen in any place of public amusement. To explain this enigma, even the conjecture of a recent writer[1] has gained some credit, who pretends that Rembrandt abandoned his fortune to Manasseh ben Israel and Ephraim Bonus to make experiments in alchemy. I think I may reject this conjecture as absurd, seeing that it does not rest on the slightest proof.

Rembrandt certainly knew these two men, one of whom acquired a reputation in theology and the other in medicine; but there is nothing to prove that these two worthy Israelites ever practised the senseless art of alchemy, or that Rembrandt ever assisted them in such a pursuit.

Rembrandt's ruin, it seems to me, may be explained in a very natural and probable manner. After the first half of the seventeenth century, the treasury of the State, exhausted by war, was in a pitiable condition ; and commerce, the nerve of the country, had also suffered great losses during the war. These were felt above all in Amsterdam, where, in 1653, there were, according to some writers, fifteen hundred, and, according to others, nearly

---

[1] Smith. *Catalogue raisonné of the Works of the most Eminent Painters, &c.* Vol. VII. p. xxvii.

three thousand empty houses. Two years later, Holland, on account of her great expenses and continual losses, was obliged to reduce the interest of her debt from five to four per cent. The effect of this reduction was long felt. Doubtless this state of things must have exercised a grievous reaction on the arts, causing works of art to be much lowered in value. Assuredly no one thought of ordering new pictures, for they are not amongst the necessaries of life. Add to this, that Rembrandt, by reason of the second marriage which he probably contracted about this period, was forced, according to Saskia Uilenburg's will, to give up to his son the whole of the maternal inheritance, whilst his own property, valued some years before at more than forty thousand florins, only produced, when it came to be sold, a little more than a quarter of that sum, on account of the badness of the times. According to the inventory of it, which still exists,[1] he had collected a large number of paintings, engravings, and drawings by the principal masters, as well as armour, antiquities, and rarities, the purchase of which had assuredly cost him dear. When all this had again to be sold, in order to fulfil the clauses of the will, the sale produced much less than the value of these objects, and decidedly very much less than they had cost. If Rembrandt had had the good fortune of Rubens, who also sold his collection during his lifetime, he would have passed the remainder of his days in affluence.

The misfortune which fell upon Rembrandt did not, however, take away his courage, nor prevent him from setting to work again and continuing with zeal his interrupted labours. Several of his admirable productions prove this.[2] Such is the salutary power of art, which, like science, is an honour in prosperity, and a refuge and consolation in misfortune. This consolation, assuredly, was not wanting to Rembrandt when he saw himself unrecognized, owing to the jealousy of his rivals and brothers in art, who, unable to

[1] A translation is given in the Appendix.
[2] Tosi, in his *Catalogue of Rembrandt's Works* (in Dutch), p. 11 of the Preface, points out the etchings which he made in the year of his disaster.

equal him in talent, had recourse to malevolence to lessen his reputation
and tarnish his name in various ways; at least the calumnious accusations
made against him appear to me to have had no other foundation. I have, I
think, clearly demonstrated that they are false, and in no wise to have been
deserved.

Virtue is the loveliest crown of true merit, and there is no just reason
for refusing the possession of this high distinction to Rembrandt. We will not
deprive him of this bright palm, but we will reinstate him in the possession of
his honour, of which he has been so audaciously robbed by envy and jealousy;
nor will we hesitate to add to our admiration of his talent, our esteem
and respect for the man.

But it is less the good qualities of the man, whatever estimate we form of
these, than the admirable merits of the painter, which we are here called upon
to consider. I proposed to myself to draw your attention particularly to this
point, for the following reason. It has often been asked, to which of his masters in painting or drawing did Rembrandt owe his rapid progress and happy
development? I willingly admit that their teaching had a salutary influence on
his first formation; but the reason that Rembrandt attained to such a high
degree of eminence in the artistic world was only owing, it is my conviction,
to himself, and himself alone. Genius is not formed according to determined
principles, nor constrained by outward rules. It trusts its own strength, and,
choosing its own road, marches courageously forward, free, and master of all its
movements. Rembrandt had not received a learned education, he had had no
celebrated masters to smooth the road towards the temple of art, and artistic
Italy had never opened for him her treasures of painting and sculpture. He
knew little of books or theoretical works on art; but he had read in the great
Book of Nature, and had seized its true sense. In this book it was that he
studied the eternal and unchangeable laws of life, and of the action of light
and shade; and by means of an attentive observation, and an exact conception
of all which surrounded him, he applied these laws in a most masterly

manner; his piercing eye penetrated the inmost secrets of Nature, and no painter ever seized her true meaning more closely, or divined it more happily in giving to the productions of art the appearance of reality.

He was, then, indebted to himself, more than to any other artist, for what he achieved, and his panegyrist proclaimed the truth when he said that " Rembrandt could only have been produced by Rembrandt."[1]

We know that Rembrandt had two different manners. The more detailed manner, resembling somewhat that which Frans Van Mieris followed, seems to belong to the first portion of his life. Afterwards, until his latter years, he adopted the broader and bolder touch by which several of his portraits are distinguished. We may note two examples of his first manner in the Royal Museum at the Hague, and two of his second manner in the museum at Amsterdam.[2]

At the museum at the Hague is the wonderful painting representing *Simeon in the Temple*, at the moment when, having taken the infant Jesus in his arms, he gives utterance to the famous canticle. By the side of Simeon we see, besides other persons, Mary and Joseph, the latter of whom holds in his hand the two doves destined for the offering. In the background a crowd of Jews are assembled around the High Priest. Whilst regarding this picture, we feel transported in imagination to the temple at Jerusalem, we take part in the ceremony, and involuntarily join in the song of Simeon. This exquisite painting is dated 1631. It is light in tone, noble in its rendering, and delicate in its execution.[3]

In the same style, but on a larger scale, is *The Lesson in Anatomy*, in which

---

[1] Immerzeel: *Eulogium of Rembrandt.*

[2] " Rembrandt may be admired in all the galleries of Europe," says Arsène Houssaye, " but we must go to the Hague and Amsterdam to salute his genius. *The Lesson in Anatomy* and *The Night-Watch* are the most striking and most eloquent expression of his two manners."

[3] *The Simeon* and all the other pictures here spoken of above are minutely described in the MUSÉES DE LA HOLLANDE, *Amsterdam and La Haye*. By W. B.

the figures are the size of life, and represented to the knees. This picture, painted a year after the *Simeon*, represents the celebrated Professor Nikolas Tulp giving a lesson in anatomy to seven pupils on a corpse extended before him. The general execution is very careful, and the subject is rendered with the strictest truth. The first look we cast on the corpse causes us a shuddering sensation of disgust; but when we afterwards examine the learned Tulp, whose eyes sparkle with life, and whose lips seem to move; and his auditors, who, recognizing the importance of his explanations, are listening with profound attention to the professor's words; we find words fail us in which properly to extol the genius of a painter who has shown us so truly, life side by side with death.

Of the two pictures in Rembrandt's broad manner exhibited here at Amsterdam in the National Museum, the one dated 1642 has a special renown. This composition is celebrated all over the world by the name of *The Night-Watch* (de Nacht-Wacht).[1] We see in it a company of citizens, who with their captain, the Chevalier Frans Banning Kok, of Pommerland and Ilpendam, and their Lieutenant, Willem van Ruytenburg, of Vlaardingen, are setting forth on some shooting expedition. One of the armed bourgeois is loading his arquebuse, another wears a crown of oak-leaves on his helmet, and, in the first sketch, a boy runs up to him with a powder-flask. Amongst the moving multitude we see a young girl, in festal array, who carries a white cock attached to her belt, probably designed for the victor. This incomparable work has already gained universal admiration on account of the excellence of its arrangement and the extraordinary force of its execution, by means of which the painter, by apparently slight effort, has produced the most striking effect. A competent judge[2] has most justly said, " Rembrandt's Night-Watch, without exaggeration, is, as a production of art, one of the marvels of the world, and the Museum of Amsterdam may well be proud of it."

---

[1] A small copy of this painting is in the National Gallery, No. 289.—ED.

[2] Nieuwenhuys: *A Review of the Lives and Works of the most Eminent Painters.*

Although less rich in composition, the second picture preserved at the Amsterdam Museum does not fall short of the first in its power and truth. This work, painted in the year 1661, represents a meeting of Syndics, (*Staalmeesters*). Four of these gentlemen are seated round a table covered with a red cloth, on which lies an open book : the fifth has risen; behind them stands a sixth person, probably a servant, with his head uncovered. They appear to be deliberating on the affairs of their administration, and are all looking up attentively, as if some one had unexpectedly appeared to them. As to the distinctive character of this painting, it is the same as with all Rembrandt's. We feel more than we can describe. Enter a rich collection of pictures, where amongst many *chefs-d'œuvre*, there is some one production of Rembrandt's brush, and involuntarily, your look will be attracted towards it, without your being able to give any account to yourself of your impression.

Rembrandt left several celebrated pupils. Gerard Douw, Ferdinand Bol, Govert Flinck, and Gerbrand Van der Eeckhout, have obtained an undoubtedly high position as painters. But although formed in his school and penetrated by his ideas and principles, they have not entirely seized and rendered one peculiar originality of their master,—an originality the cause of which must be sought, not in the secret of his manner of working, as is ordinarily asserted, but in the secret of his Genius.

In the opinion of able connoisseurs, Rembrandt's merit consists above all in striking effects, vigorous colour, and masterly execution. As I said just now, he studied Nature most attentively, and carefully observed the action of light on colour. This study led him to make a special theory of light and colours, which, applied with judgment, enabled him to reproduce in his works those fantastic effects which many have imitated, but none have ever equalled.

His figures do not seem laid on the canvas; they come out from it and advance towards us in a living form. Rembrandt knew better than any other painter the art of placing objects in the fullest daylight, and, without exaggeration, making their colours speak. He knew how to seize the moment when Nature is most picturesque, and with a light hand reproduced her fresh tints on his canvas. His colour is so beautiful, that, in this respect, he equals, if he does not surpass, the great Titian, who has often been called the father of colour. To this he joined a happy harmony of tone and arrangement. The disposition of his subjects is generally rich and always well considered. He troubled himself very little about costume, so that in his pictures we often find the costumes of the east and west mixed up together, or allied in the most whimsical manner ; but certainly he did not act thus without meaning it to tell well on the whole.

The same excuse may be alleged if he sometimes departed from the ordinary rules of drawing in order to follow at his own will and caprice the inspiration which moved him. It is owing to his fidelity to Nature that we sometimes meet with it in him under its less noble forms. He did not strive after the ideal in his pictures, as is the tendency of the Italian school, and he has proved that, even without the admixture of the ideal, painting may fulfil its high mission, simply by the expression of reality. In short, his conception and execution are alike superior, and rarely, in any of his works, however small, or of however little importance, do we not find originality of idea with perfection in execution.

I should be doing wrong to Rembrandt's genius if I passed by in silence his celebrated etchings ; for he shone no less as an etcher than as a painter. The same original theory of light and colour which he followed in his painting, he applied also to his engraving. He painted, so to speak, on the copper, and gave to his works in aquafortis, as well as to his paintings, the vigour and distinctness to which they owe their brilliancy and softness of tone. He seems sometimes to have played with his point, yet nevertheless he never traced an unintentional line, or made a useless stroke. All his works bear the marks of just conception and profound reflection. The limits of my plan do not permit me to give many examples of his talent as an etcher, but I cannot help citing two. I intentionally choose two subjects taken from Holy Writ. There it was that he expressed himself most forcibly—in order to demonstrate the talent he possessed of rendering apparent in the most striking manner the most opposite impressions and situations.

The first of these etchings represents *Christ healing the Sick.* The Saviour stands in a very dignified attitude, in the middle of a crowd of sick people, who have run to him to implore his miraculous assistance for their cure. His left arm rests on a stone,[1] whilst in speaking to the people he stretches forth his right hand. The sick are depicted in the most touching manner, their faces and their bodies are fleshless, and their eyes are weary. Yet, nevertheless, we read in them, and their attitudes also show, that their trust is in Him from whom alone they hope for cure and salvation. On the right side are seen several Jews, attracted there, probably, by curiosity and the hope of being present at a miracle.

The other etching is not less noble in conception. It represents the *Death of Mary.* The Virgin mother is lying on a bed dying. The faithful Joseph, standing by, has his arm around her, and is endeavouring to reanimate the vital powers which are on the point of being extinguished. Near him a doctor holds Mary's hand, and attentively calculates the beating of her pulse. On the other side of the bed is seated a priest, with an open book before him : he has ceased reading, and, as well as the high priest placed in front of him, is looking at Mary with interest. Farther back are several women weeping or praying. And, whilst all are surrounding the bed with expressions of deep grief, waiting for the last sigh of the dying one—above, the heavens are opened, and a choir of cherubin descend towards the mother of our Lord, to bear her away to the region of eternity.

---

[1] This was the first intention, of which traces are still seen in the first states of the etching. But in one of those alterations so common with Rembrandt, he straightened the left arm and raised the hand as if with a gesture of preaching. The figure of Christ, so majestically simple, has gained movement by this. W. B.

But when should we finish if we desired to point out all the beauties of
Rembrandt's works? How should I be able to follow this prodigious genius
in his bold course—in his elevated flights? I recognize his merit as being
far above my praise. Do you desire a better panegyrist? the discourse of the
learned Immerzeel will furnish you with it; but the best eulogium on the talent
of the incomparable Rembrandt you will find in his own works. Go and
stand before one of his masterly paintings, and if you have any feeling for the
truly beautiful, if one spark of pure taste warms and animates your heart, you
will acknowledge that he who has executed such great things merits the
admiration not only of his own countrymen but the whole world, and that
he is worthy of the homage of a grateful posterity.

Ten years ago, when a monument was raised to Hadrianus Junius, in the
church of the capital of Zealand, I had the honour of receiving from the
Academy of Sciences at Middleburg, an invitation to deliver a discourse
on the day of the inauguration of the Cenotaph, on the 20th April, 1842.
I responded to this request by reading a short address, in which I viewed
the distinction accorded to the celebrated Junius—who, with Erasmus, was
the most learned Netherlander of his time, and who has been called by some
the light of Holland, and by others the ornament of his age—as being not
only a testimony of respect for his literary merit in particular, but as being at
the same time a recognition of that of our ancestors in general. If on that
occasion I was happy to be able to render homage to Science, it is quite as
flattering to me to-day to have a like task confided to me with respect to Art,
represented by the great Rembrandt. Where is the man who, loving his
country, does not attach the highest importance to the study of Science as the
first and necessary condition of all civilization? or, who does not strive, as
much as lies in his power, to favour the interests of Art, whose powerful
influence embellishes and ennobles the life of the people? Perhaps our fathers
have shone in none of the arts more than in painting, and assuredly no

one in our country has surpassed that prince among artists, the immortal Rembrandt.

Rembrandt may then legitimately aspire to the honour so justly intended for him : and rightly has a meeting of the true patrons of art decided that Holland, which has enjoyed for two centuries the lustre of Rembrandt's glory, and which proudly places his name side by side with those of Rubens and of Raphael, owes him a mark of her highest recognition and a durable proof of her gratitude

From more recent investigations in the archives of Amsterdam, Dr. Scheltema has discovered the following documentary evidence regarding Rembrandt :—

In the Register of Baptisms in the Old Church (*Oude Kerk*). "On Friday evening, 30th October, 1654, Cornelia, the daughter of Rembrandt van Reyn and Hendricktie Stoffels, was presented for baptism ; Witness, Anne Jans."

In the Register of Deaths (*Doodboek*) of the West Church (*Wester Kerk*), beneath the entry of the death of Rembrandt, " Tuesday, 8th October, 1669, Rembrandt van Ryn, painter, of the Roosegraft, opposite the Doolhof, leaving two children," we read " 21st December, 1674, Catherina van Wyck, the widow, has declared that she has no means of proving that her

children had anything to inherit from their father: of the truth of which
Catherina Thennis Blanckerhoff, the aunt, is witness. Present, M. Hinlopen."

It appears, then, that Rembrandt must have had three wives: Saskia
Uilenburg, from 1634 to 1642, by whom he had four children; Rombertus,
baptized on the 15th of December, 1635, when Jan Cornelius Silvius and his
wife, who was a cousin of Saskia, were witnesses; Cornelia, baptized on the
22nd of July, 1638, in the presence of "Dominicus Johannes Silvius;"
(this child died in the following month;) Cornelia, baptized on the 29th of
July, 1640, in the presence of Commissioner Francoys Copal and Titia van
Uylenburg; Titus, baptized on the 22nd of September, 1641, in the presence
of Secretary Gerard van Loo, Commissioner Copal, and Aeltgen Pieters the
widow of Johannes Silvius. The three first were baptized in the Oude Kerk,
and all died young.

Titus was baptized in the Zuider Kerk (South Church) and lived to
the age of 27. He married, in February, 1668, his cousin by his mother's
side, Magdalena van Loo; but he died in September of the same year, just
thirteen months before his illustrious father. In March, 1669, the widow
of Titus gave birth to a child, who was christened Titia. The mother died
thirteen days after her father-in-law, Rembrandt; so that the poor child, who
never knew a father, lost her mother and her grandfather before she was
eight months old. This Titia van Rhyn married a young jeweller named
Van Bijler, who lived in Amsterdam, where she died in November, 1725.

By his second wife, Hendrikje, Rembrandt had one child christened, in
1654, Cornelia. And by his third wife, Catharina, he had in his last years,
at least the two children whom he left "without inheritance" at his death.

ON THE ETCHINGS OF REMBRANDT.

E

ON THE ETCHINGS OF REMBRANDT.

F the inestimable value of Rembrandt's Etchings, as works of art, we need no greater proof than that afforded by the great number of criticisms which have been at various times published concerning them. Essays have been written on them in Holland and Germany, France and England, and always with the same amount of admiration and praise. Collectors of Rembrandt's Etchings, from the time of the Burgomaster Six to our own days, have found the greatest delight in gathering together these celebrated productions, and no amateur has been contented until he has added some examples of Rembrandt's works to his portfolio.

After so much has been said concerning the art-merits of these works it is needless to enter into fresh discussions ; but as the books in which many of these criticisms appeared are now very scarce, the republication of a few of the best notices will be a matter of interest to those who have not access to the originals.

We will first quote from Adam Bartsch, an engraver by profession, and Keeper of the Print Room in the Museum in Vienna, who, in the year 1797, wrote thus :—

"However great may be the reputation that Rembrandt has acquired by his paintings, he is no less celebrated for his Etchings, which have at all times excited the admiration of connoisseurs. Three hundred and seventy-six different pieces of his are known, of which one hundred and

seventy-three bear the date of the year in which they were done, the others
being without date. The oldest are of the year 1628, and the latest of 1661.
According to these dates Rembrandt did not commence engraving until
he was twenty-two years of age, and only gave up the graver thirteen
years before his death.[1] It is true, that amongst his undated prints there may
be some that were done before the first, or after the last of these epochs; but
they are all so equal in merit, and of such great perfection, that it is difficult
to point out one which bears the marks of the inexperience of youth or the
feebleness of old age.

With the exception of the colouring, all that we have said of the
beauties and imperfections of Rembrandt's paintings applies equally well to
his engravings. They are in the same manner admirable and defective; but
their beauties strike us so forcibly that we scarcely heed their defects. A
vagabond liberty, a picturesque disorder, an easy touch, the rarest perception
of *chiar' oscuro*, and the talent of expressing the character of the different
ages and subjects which he was treating, by touches thrown in as it were by
chance; such are some of the elements, and there are many more which
constitute the merit of Rembrandt as an engraver, which give such an
inexpressible charm to his prints.

Rembrandt would never etch in any person's presence; so that most
of his processes have long been regarded as impenetrable secrets. Several
artists have tried to imitate them, and have succeeded in some, but have never
found out the whole. It is certain that Rembrandt's prints, considered only
in regard to their engraving, independently of their design and *chiar' oscuro*,
have a character which is quite peculiar to him. The execution of his copper-
plates is sometimes rough and sometimes finished, but the lines always cross
each other in such different directions that it is impossible to follow them, as
we can in most of the prints of other engravers. Nevertheless we cannot be

---

[1] Since Bartsch's time it has been ascertained that Rembrandt was born in July, 1606, and died
in October, 1669.—ED.

of Houbraken's opinion, who says that there is now no means of finding out
the artifices employed by Rembrandt in his engraving; that they are buried
with their inventor in the same way as the art of painting on glass, as it was
exercised by Dirk and Wonter Crabet[1] has been lost with them. We, however, are persuaded, on the contrary, that the only real secret of Rembrandt's
engraving lay in his genius, and that his processes may nearly all be explained.
This is the result of the researches that we have made on this subject.[2]

Except in portraits, Rembrandt scarcely ever chalked the outlines of
his designs. He drew them at once on the plate with the same freedom
and disorder as one meets with in his rough pen-and-ink sketches.

This manner of projecting his subjects on to the plate is shown in several
of his prints; *The Drawer of the Model* is the most striking example of
it. This was not certainly the way to produce a correct design, but it was
a sure means of preserving all the fire of the first conception. He very often
touched up his plates with aquafortis. The first operation was only of use in
bringing out the most delicate work. He then varnished the plate a second
time, increasing the force of the work by adding new hatchings and again
employing aquafortis.

By this process he obtained tender tones in the light parts, delicacy in
fine details, and strength in the shadows, without getting the lines confused.
In order to have proof of these sort of touchings up with aquafortis the
portrait of *Rembrandt* (No. 7) may be consulted amongst others. The folds
of the frill round the neck, which are scarcely visible in the first proof,
are well expressed in the second, where they have been strengthened by
a second operation of aquafortis. In examining *The Good Samaritan* one
sees that the principal shadows of the dog have been fortified by the same
means. This piece shows likewise that Rembrandt, in order to obtain variety

---

[1] *Groote Schouburgh, etc.* Part I. p. 271.
[2] John Burnet, in " Rembrandt and his Works," (p. 33), has described Rembrandt's process of
etching.

in his tones, not only employed points of different degrees of sharpness, but that also during the operation of the aquafortis he successively covered his plates with an unctuous substance, in order to produce different degrees of depth in his work.

Rembrandt was very skilful in the use of the dry-point. There are but few of his engravings in which one does not remark its more or less constant employment. *The Annunciation to the Shepherds*, the portrait of *Abraham Frans*, that of *Young Haaring*, and many other pieces, have been entirely worked up with this tool, which has produced the most beautiful effect. He often sketched out his engravings with aquafortis in a light manner and with simple and broad work. He afterwards covered them abundantly with cross hatchings with the dry-point and the burin, giving them by this means a very finished air, full of effect and warmth.

The portrait of *Dr. Faustus*, which Rembrandt has not entirely finished, is a proof of this process. The table, the books upon it, the globe, and even the head of Faustus, were in aquafortis, and simply sketched ; all these objects being intended to be worked up with more effect in the same way as the background, which is the only part quite finished. In the *Christ Healing the Sick* there is scarcely anything except the contours of the figures etched in aquafortis, all the *chiar' oscuro*, which is so much admired, is for the most part the work of the fine and close hatchings of the dry-point. In this magnificent piece in particular Rembrandt has exhibited the art of employing this implement for glazing and for producing all sorts of tints.

The portrait of *Van Coppenol* offers a similar example. In the first proof of this print the right arm and the hand are only lightly sketched in aquafortis ; the second proof shows these same parts well worked up with the dry-point and the whole of the dark background added with this tool alone. One can really hardly conceive how Rembrandt was able to produce such dark brown tones by the simple use of the dry-point, or how it was possible to extend these tones in such large masses; however, it is very certain that he did so, and any one may convince himself of the fact by attentively observing the prints we have mentioned. But that which chiefly proves the amount of skill and firmness which Rembrandt brought to the use of the dry-point, is a *Landscape* (No.222), which he executed entirely by its means, without employing aquafortis at all. Even his name and the year 1652 are engraved in this way, notwithstanding the obstacle presented in the forms of the letters. In examining this landscape, one is astonished at the facility which distinguished it, and which seems so opposed to the use of a tool which is so greatly hindered by the resistance of the metal. It is to be thought that Rembrandt made use of an extremely sharp dry-point, and that he leant on the copper with the greatest force. The first proof of the *Ecce Homo* presents lines drawn the whole length of the plate and accompanied by strong *burrs*.[1] The latter prove the depth of the lines and the force which Rembrandt used in cutting the copper.

The burin was another implement which Rembrandt used with the same success as the dry-point, although less frequently. He generally employed it when he wished to mark his shadows with light touches, or when he desired to produce an intensity which could not be obtained by means of aquafortis and the dry-point. The *Ecce Homo* and *The Descent from the Cross* have both been greatly touched up with the burin.

On these occasions he made use of the burin as a painter, that is to say, he intermixed its work with that of the aquafortis, with such wonderful skill, that it is scarcely possible to distinguish the one from the other. So various were his processes that several pieces exist which have been entirely engraved with the burin. *The Model Drawer* is amongst this number. All the shadows are executed with the burin in fine cuttings, closely crossed and lying one over the other. In order to make them as black as possible, and, to give unity to the whole, Rembrandt worked it up with the dry-point,

[1] The *burr* is caused by the rough edge of the copper standing up where the tool has cut the metal.

crossed and recrossed the hatchings in every possible way, until he obtained the desired tones.

The Gold Weigher appears to be engraved in this manner, and the portrait of the *Burgomaster Six* bears but few traces of aquafortis; nearly all the shadows in it are done with the burin, and afterwards passed over and glazed with the dry-point. Rembrandt, whose great practice in the working of aquafortis made him so perfectly well acquainted with its effects, was not ignorant that it was not possible, by its use alone, to produce narrow hatchings composed of strokes both fine and deep at the same time. He therefore renounced aquafortis whenever he wished to produce a fine velvety and vigorous appearance, persuaded that the burin alone could give this. That is why the most vigorous proof of the copy done in aquafortis by Basan of the Burgomaster Six appears crude, cold, and grey in comparison with the original print, even when the latter has not the highest degree of brilliancy, as is the case with the impression which is now in the Imperial Library of Vienna.

Aiming at painting rather than engraving his plates, Rembrandt followed none of the ordinary rules of engravers, but employed, as we have shown, any manner and any process which his genius told him would produce the desired effect. He put such complicated work into some of his etchings, that it could hardly be developed. It is with great difficulty, for instance, that one can explain in what mode he has engraved *The Flight into Egypt.* It is certain that the grey tone in the first proof of this piece, which is spread over the group and the rising ground on which the group is placed, is only the effect of the pumice-stone with which these places have been rubbed; but it is not so easy to give an account of the process employed on the landscape which occupies the left side of this print. There are scarcely any lines to be discovered in it, and the few one finds appear as if they were traced over it afterwards. All the foliage consists of an assemblage of points more or less close together and very different in form and colour, according as the aquafortis has operated with greater or less strength. If, whilst varnishing a plate preparatory to etching it in aquafortis, the scraper be leant on rather heavily, it results, on raising it, that the varnish is found pierced with an infinite number of little holes, especially if it has already begun to cool. The varnish in this state exactly resembles the dotting of the foliage in the print we have mentioned, and we are tempted to believe that Rembrandt has made effective use of this manœuvre, and that the large masses of foliage already perhaps expressed in a great measure by the chance movement of the scraper have been perfected in a second operation by preserving the lights from the effects of the aquafortis by means of a brush dipped into a liquid varnish. But this view we only advance as a conjecture, leaving its probability to be judged of by those of our readers who are acquainted with the art of engraving. We shall be content if we have thrown any light on the other artifices and manœuvres employed by Rembrandt in engraving his plates, and with having by this means rendered some useful assistance to those who are striving to imitate the charming style of this incomparable artist.

There also exists a wood-engraving by Rembrandt, representing the bust of a philosopher. If there were several pieces executed in this style of engraving amongst Rembrandt's works, the question might be mooted as to whether Rembrandt engraved them himself, or whether he merely furnished the design. For it is not likely that this fiery artist, who flew, so to speak, from one plate to another, without having the patience to finish them, should ever have had a taste for a kind of engraving so contrary to his ardent genius, and which, by the slow mechanism that it requires, seems to belong rather to a cold artisan. But this piece being very small, and the only one there is by him, it may be believed that for a whim he executed it himself.

Rembrandt frequently took a few proofs on Chinese paper of his plates. These are much sought after, and always preferred to those on ordinary paper, not only because the yellow colour of this paper gives them a more harmonious appearance, but also because they were the first taken.

F

There are also some proofs on parchment; but although these are first proofs they are not sought after so eagerly, for they are generally badly printed, and the parchment, being liable to shrivel up, nearly always leaves striking unevennesses, which it is never possible to smooth out."

John Smith, in his well-known Catalogue Raisonné of the works of the Dutch Painters, says: "There is a department of art which Rembrandt carried to such perfection that, as it admits of no comparison with any other, he stands alone in it, unequalled and unrivalled;—namely, his wonderful productions in EAU FORTE. His taste for etching appears to have been almost coeval with the use of the palette, and his fondness for it as an amusement, must have occupied a large portion of his leisure hours. Not a year passed after his commencement as a painter, without one or more beautiful productions emanating from his burin, until he had sent forth to the world about three hundred and sixty-five prints. In this pursuit he appears to be singularly careful to throw off a few impressions in the various states of his plate, and in numerous instances, after making the most trifling alterations; this propensity he carried so far, that, in a few instances, he has touched on finished works, so as to destroy in some measure the beauty they previously possessed. These trials and alterations in his plates could not always have been done for the purpose of essaying their state, he must have had some ulterior object in view, and this could have been nothing else than to promote an increased sale of impressions in the various states of his plates. Whatever benefit he may have derived from this innocent artifice, he could little have foreseen the consequences of thus multiplying his etchings on the amateur world, nor could it have entered into his conception that a print of the value of a few stuivers, would, in the process of time, sell for sixty guineas; or a portrait of his friend Tolling, value perhaps five florins, fetch, at a public sale, 130 guineas; or that the piece, representing *Christ Healing the Sick*, which, for its singular excellence, sold, on one occasion for 100 guilders, about £8 12s, the usual price being 45 florins, and thereby obtained the cognomen of The Hundred Guilder Print, would at length sell for 250 guineas.

" These precious productions of the burin appear to have cost him no previous study or labour in preparing the compositions; for, with the exception of three or four instances, no pictures or drawings exist corresponding with the prints. The plate appears to have been taken in hand, and, to the superficial observer, a confusion of lines made, crossing each other in all directions; out of this seeming chaos, his ready invention conceived, and his dexterous hand embodied, the subject, which a little labour afterwards carried to perfection: hence these excellent productions may, with propriety, be considered drawings or pictures, for they possess the same powerful expression, and have, to a certain extent, the same properties, as brilliancy of effect, richness of tone, and freedom of hand. Of his readiness and dexterity in the performance of these works, some idea may be formed from an anecdote given by most of his biographers. 'Being at table with his constant friend and patron, the Burgomaster Six, the mustard was asked for, and it not being on the table, the servant went to fetch it. Rembrandt, knowing the tardiness of this domestic, laid a wager with his friend, that he would commence and finish an etching before he returned. This he actually performed, and the plate is known under the appellation of *Six's Bridge* ; or, the *Mustard-Pot.*

" To acquire a correct knowledge of these etchings, together with their numerous variations, demands the study and application of years, and few may be said to be perfect masters of it, for new variations are constantly being discovered. In this pursuit, the labours of the amateur are, in some measure, abridged by the Catalogues Raisonnées, which have at various times been published, each succeeding one being more complete than the former. Of these, Gersaint's appeared in 1752. A Supplement to the same, by Pierre Yver, in 1756. Daulby's, in 1796. Bartsch's, in 1797. M. le Chevalier de Claussin's, in 1824; to which he added a Supplement in 1828."[1]

[1] M. Charles Blanc published his " L'Œuvre Complet de Rembrandt " in 1859.

We will next quote from the well-known engraver, John Burnet, who says, " The portrait of the *Burgomaster Six* is the most finished and perfect of all the etchings of Rembrandt ; and as it was done expressly for his friend and patron, we can easily imagine that the painter exerted himself to the utmost, so as to render it worthy of the subject. I have been at some trouble to get an account of the family of Jan Six, but have gleaned little from those books connected with the history of Holland. During the war with England, in the reign of Charles the Second, he was Secretary of State to the City of Amsterdam, and his family was afterwards connected with some of their most celebrated men. But what has rendered his name more famous than intermarrying with the families of Van Tromp or De Ruyter, is his patronage of Rembrandt—in the same way that Lord Southampton's name is ennobled by his patronage of Shakespeare. We know he was devoted to literature as well as the fine arts, having left a tragedy on the story of Medea, a copy of which is mentioned in the catalogue of Rembrandt's effects, and an etching by the artist was prefixed to the work—viz. the *Marriage of Jason and Creusa ;* the rare states of this print are before the quotation of the Dutch verses underneath, also the statue of Juno is without the diadem, which was afterwards added. I have mentioned that this portrait was a private plate ; in fact, the copper is still in possession of the family. In a sale which took place in 1734, for a division of the property among the various branches, fourteen impressions were sold, but brought comparatively small prices, from the number to be contended for. Two proofs, however, on India paper are still in the portfolio of his descendants, which in five years will, it is said, be brought to the hammer, as by that time the parties will be of age. These proofs will in all probability realize two hundred guineas each. The ease and natural attitude of the figure in this work are admirable ; the intensity of the light, with the delicacy and truth of the reflected lights, are rendered with the strong stamp of genius ; the diffusion of the light also, by means of the papers on the chair, and the few sparkling touches in the shadow, completely take this etching out of the catalogue of common portraiture. The only work that I can at present think of that can be brought into competition with it, is the full-length portrait of *Charles the First*, by Vandyke, in the Queen's Collection, and which is rendered so familiar by Strange's admirable engraving.

In entering into an examination of the execution of this print, it is evident the whole effect is produced by means of the dry-point, which must have been a work of great labour. The best impressions are on India paper ; and I perceive, by referring to Gersaint's catalogue, that at the sale of the Burgomaster's property, they only brought about eighteen florins. The next portrait amongst his etchings that at all approaches to the Burgomaster, is that of *Old Haarin*, which has always struck me as one of the foundations for the style of Sir Joshua Reynolds in portraiture. A fine impression of this work on India paper, is more like Sir Joshua than many prints after his own pictures ; and with all the high veneration I have for Reynolds, I cannot omit noticing how very ambiguously he frequently speaks of this great genius. We know his master, Hudson, had an excellent collection of Rembrandt's works, and therefore he must have been early imbued with their merits and peculiarities. This, however, we shall have a better opportunity of noticing when we come to the treatment of colour. The next etching in excellence I should mention is the portrait of *John Lutma, the Goldsmith*, with the light background ; this was afterwards softened down by the introduction of a window. And here I must observe, that though he often had light backgrounds to his prints, yet in his finished pictures they were generally the reverse. The etching of *Ephraim Bonus, the Jewish Physician*, is also one of his most effective works ; the introduction of the balustrade, on which he leans descending the staircase, removes it from the ordinary level of mere portraiture. On the hand that rests upon the balustrade, is a ring, which in the very rare impressions, from its being done with the dry-point, prints dark from the burr. These are invaluable, as in that state the whole work has the fulness and richness of a picture. A very large sum was given for the impression of the print in this state—now in the British Museum—in fact, one hundred and sixty pounds ; though at the Verstolke sale, where this print was purchased, the commission given amounted to two hundred and fifty pounds : but when we consider that the collection in the British Museum is now the finest in existence, no extra price should be spared to complete the collection, especially as these works are foundations for the sure improvement of the fine arts in the country. The crown jewels are exhibited as a necessary appendage to the rank of the nation—but there the value stops ; now the works of art in this country are not only valuable, but intrinsically beneficial. We know that Charles the Second pawned the crown pearls to the Dutch for a few thousands ; but our collection of Rembrandts would realize in Holland at least ten thousand pounds. This, of course, is a digression, and is merely mentioned here to show how absurd the hue and cry is, that the country is wasting money in purchasing a few specimens of fine art. The portrait of *Utenbogardus* is also excellent ; and I here may notice the large book, which Rembrandt was so fond of introducing, as a means of a breadth of light and employment for his portraits. Now, to these circumstances we are indebted for some of the finest works of both Reynolds and Lawrence : amongst many, I might mention the large ledger in Lawrence's portraits of the *Baring Family*, and Sir Joshua's picture of the *Dilettante Society*, and others. No doubt we find these means of making up a picture both in Raffaelle and Titian ; but it is rendered more applicable to our own purposes when it is brought nearer to our own times, especially when translated by so great a genius as Rembrandt. The next fine work amongst his etchings is the portrait of *Cornelius Silvius*, the head of which, being delicately finished with the dry needle, is seldom seen very fine. This also has a book, and the hand extended beyond the frame of the oval opening, upon which it casts its shadow. This practice of representing objects nearer the eye than the frame is certainly to be observed in some of the prints after Rubens and others, and has descended to several common prints in our own time, but ought not to be adopted, as bordering too much upon that art which may be designated as a sort of *ad captandum vulgus* display. As we shall speak more particularly of Rembrandt's portraits when colour is investigated, these works are merely mentioned as excellent specimens of composition and chiaro-scuro. I must not omit, however, to notice here the great *Coppenol*, the writing-master to the city of Amsterdam; he holds a pen and a sheet of paper in his hand, and is looking at the spectator with a look of intelligent observation. The head and figure of this work were perfected, in the first instance, before the background was put in, and in this state is exceedingly rare—the one in the British Museum is valued at five hundred guineas, and was left, amongst other rare works in his collection, by the Rev. Mr. Cracherode, to the public. And here we ought to bear in mind, when individuals contribute so largely by their bequests to the country, it is our bounden duty to carry out their views by perfecting the various collections as opportunities offer in the course of time, which to them was impossible. In one of the impressions in the Museum, in a finished state, is written, in a large ornamental hand, a commendation by Coppenol himself, wherein he says he does so to unite his name with that of the great artist, Rembrandt Van Ryn, as by that means he knows he shall secure immortality to himself. The portrait, however, that is the most powerful, as well as the most rare, is *Van Tolling, the Advocate.* The effect, both from the reflected light on the face, and the fearless masses of burr, is more like a picture than a print, and renders every other etching comparatively tame. From the chemical bottles at the side, and from the character of the gown in which he is dressed, I am of opinion that he was a physician. The excellence of this work, added to its rarity, has at all times produced large prices. There are two states of this print—the first with an irregular beard, the second with the beard cut square, also some additional work on the drapery, &c; but, what is worthy of remark is, in both states it is exceedingly scarce; in fact, there are but seven impressions known—viz. two in the British

Museum, one in Mr. Holford's collection, one in Mr. Hawkins', in Amsterdam one, in Paris one, and one in the collection of Mr. Rudge. I ought here to notice that the *Van Tolling* is one of the prints bequeathed to the nation by the Rev. Mr. Cracherode, and that at the sale of the Hon. Pole Carew's prints, in 1835, this valuable etching was purchased for the late Baron Verstolke, for two hundred and fifty pounds.

In the " Fine Arts Quarterly " of June, 1866, we find the following :— " In Rembrandt's house in the Breestraat, besides upwards of 150 pictures in oil, most of them by himself and his pupils, but some of them by Van Eyck, Raphael, Giorgione, and Michael Angelo ; besides casts from the life of whole and parts of figures and animals, statues, antique busts, arms and armour, wind and stringed instruments, zoological, mineralogical, and botanical specimens, costumes, and every conceivable accessory to artistic suggestion and production,—were found nearly one hundred volumes of the prints of all the great painter-engravers who had flourished in Europe from the discovery of the art to his own time—Schoen, the Meckens, Lucas Cranach, Lucas of Leyden, Dürer, Vandyke, Rubens, Hollar, Holbein, Jordaens, Andrea Mantegna, Bonasone, Titian, Guido, Tempesta, the Caracci, &c ; the most precious works (we quote the catalogue) of Marc Antonio, after the designs of Raphael ; together with a supplementary collection of the prints of contemporary artists, who, as they are not mentioned by name, were probably the etchers. In a word, not only a complete illustration of the engraver's art as it had been practised for 200 years, but an almost equally complete representation of Art itself, as it had existed since the revival. The Gothicism of the Germans, the academicism of the Italians, and the realism of the Flemings, had here each a fair and, as exemplified in their engraving, a more ample demonstration than they had ever received before ;—the graceful contours of Marc Antonio conveying a refined ideal of that kind of beauty which depends upon form—the complex but more dextrous curves and inflexions of Albert Dürer, not devoid of a

certain semi-barbarous expression—the noble simplicity of Andrea Mantegna
—the strength of Rubens—the weakness of Guido—the truth of Holbein—the
courtly artifice of Vandyke. Rembrandt availed himself of this vast collection
as a man who lived only for his art would. It was an open book to him to
which we find him making constant reference; at one time adding to its stores
by bidding chivalrous prices for single prints of masters with whom he might
be supposed to have little sympathy, but in whom, doubtless, he saw a quality
which he thought cheaply acquired at any price;[1] at another making elaborate
studies of subjects which interested him or which served his immediate purpose.
To this collection and to his numerous copies of the Oriental drawings which
it contained,—prompted, of course, by the innate sentiment which led him to
use them for such a purpose,—we probably owe it that of all the men who
have undertaken to illustrate the Bible, he is the only one that has been able
to give faithful expression to its simple reality and to make us personal sharers
in the homely and impressive incidents with which it abounds. Who, for
instance, that has seen that commonest of his etchings the *Return of the
Prodigal*, or that still more affecting one of *Tobit*—the stricken old man
vainly feeling for the door which is within a foot of him;—or the little subject
full of grief of the disciples carrying our Lord to the burial; or the so-called
Death of the Virgin,—the body slipping towards the foot of the bed, as dying
bodies do—without being sensible of this faculty, and of the deep natural
tenderness of character by the promptings of which alone their author could
have produced them? To the influence of Titian, again, whose drawings
Rembrandt possessed, we owe the splendid backgrounds of some and whole
subjects of others of his etchings;[2] while, in a minute copy of a morality
of Andrea Mantegna's, we have a singular proof that the quaint but impressive
work of the earliest and most simple of his predecessors was not without its
influence upon him. We have been thus particular in directing attention to

---

[1] For *The Espiegle* of Lucas Van Leyden, eighty-eight guilders.
[2] The St. Jerome with the lion and the square tower. Ch. Blanc. 75.

G

the copious use made by Rembrandt of his collection, because we wish to show that it was not without due warrant and consideration that he broke through the prescriptions of two centuries, and because it presents the great student to us in a noble aspect and in a character as far removed as possible from that of the charlatan and the cheat. Then, again, what man more competent or more likely than he—surrounded by all that was accounted great in art—to perceive and to weigh, to select and to turn to account, whatever he thought worthy his adoption, or—if he had found a better—to amend the practice he had begun in his father's mill?"

PHOTOGRAPHS OF REMBRANDT'S ETCHINGS.

THE ANGEL APPEARING TO THE SHEPHERDS.

ND there were in the same country shepherds abiding in the field, keeping watch over their flock by night. And, lo, the angel of the Lord came upon them, and the glory of the Lord shone round about them : and they were sore afraid. And the angel said unto them, Fear not: for, behold, I bring you good tidings of great joy, which shall be to all people. For unto you is born this day in the city of David, a Saviour, which is Christ the Lord. And this shall be a sign unto you; Ye shall find the babe wrapped in swaddling clothes, lying in a manger. And suddenly there was with the angel a multitude of the heavenly host, praising God, and saying, Glory to God in the highest, and on earth peace, good will toward men.—*Luke* ii. 8-14.

This is a night-piece in the country. In the middle a bridge is discovered; and on the right some trees and shrubs spring on a bank. At the top, to the left, appears a luminous space, in which a great number of cherubs are seen. Below them is an angel standing upon a cloud, with his left hand raised towards heaven, revealing to the shepherds the birth of our Lord. They appear to be astonished and terrified at the sudden light that bursts upon them; even the cattle express their fear by flight. The glory illumines the figures, the cattle, and part of the foreground, and likewise catches the extremities of the trees. This is an exceedingly fine print, and produces an admirable effect.—*Daulby, No.* 43.

There are four states of this plate. In the first, the angels, the shepherds, and the animals are but slightly sketched, and the trunk of the tree in the middle of the picture is quite white. There are but two proofs known ; one in the British Museum, from which the photograph is taken, the other in the Dresden Museum.

In the second state, the etching is more finished, but the wings and dress of the angel, and the upper part of the trunk of the tree, are still white ; and the two cows are not so much worked upon as in the third state.

In the fourth state, the trunk of the tree, and the wings and dress of the angel are all shaded.

JESUS CHRIST DRIVING THE MONEY-CHANGERS OUT
OF THE TEMPLE.

ND Jesus went into the temple of God, and cast out all them that sold and bought in the temple, and overthrew the tables of the money-changers, and the seats of them that sold doves, and said unto them, It is written, My house shall be called the house of prayer; but ye have made it a den of thieves. And the blind and the lame came to him in the temple; and he healed them.—*Matthew* xxi. 12-14.

This is a fine print, full of work, highly finished, and produces a grand effect. The architecture of the temple is richly disposed, many pillars are seen, and from the arched ceiling, on the left, is suspended a lustre. Our Saviour, from whose head proceeds a glory, is in the middle of the foreground; he has overturned a table, at which sat a money-changer, who is securing a bag with money; several pieces are sliding off the table. The man looks up with fear at our Saviour, whose left hand holds up a scourge, with which he is about to strike him. A woman, with a basket of doves on her head, with many other persons, are endeavouring to get away. To the right, all are in hurry and confusion; some are thrown down by cattle, which are making their escape. Behind them, on an elevation in the temple, is seen the high priest, with many attendants. One of them holds a crosier, and they appear to be sitting in judgment on a person who is on his knees before them. The heads of this piece are full of expression. At the bottom, to the right, is written *Rembrandt f.* 1635.—*Daulby, No.* 69.

There are two states of this plate. In the second, the mouth of the man who is dragged by the ox is larger than it is in the first state. There are a few other points of difference.

THE RESURRECTION OF LAZARUS.

HEN they took away the stone from the place where the dead was laid. And Jesus lifted up his eyes, and said, Father, I thank thee that thou hast heard me. And I knew that thou hearest me always: but because of the people which stand by, I said it, that they may believe that thou hast sent me. And when he had thus spoken, he cried with a loud voice, Lazarus, come forth. And he that was dead came forth, bound hand and foot with grave-clothes: and his face was bound about with a napkin. Jesus saith unto them, Loose him, and let him go.—*John* xi. 41-44.

This is a large arched piece, finely executed, and the *chiar'-oscuro* produces a great effect. Our Lord, who is placed a little to the left, and turned to the right, is represented standing, in a dignified attitude, on a stone, which appears to have been a part of the tomb of Lazarus. His left hand is extended above his head, and his right rests upon his side; behind him is a group of six figures, two of whom, with uplifted hands, appear terrified at the miracle. At the feet of our Lord appears Lazarus, just rising above the tomb; his death-like countenance is admirably expressive of his late situation. On the right are several figures; one of them, probably intended for his sister, stretches out her arms, and seems in haste to receive him; above her, a man (his head covered with a cap), starts back with terror and amazement. Above our Lord are some folds of drapery that form a kind of funereal canopy, within which, in the background, hang the turban and sword, with the bow and quiver of Lazarus. On the rock, opposite to the breast of our Saviour, is written *Rt. v. Ryn f.*—*Daulby, No.* 74.

M. Charles Blanc has found impressions from eleven different states of this plate, but they do not appear to differ in any important particular. It is clear that when Rembrandt wished to take great pains with an etching, he tried various effects; sometimes adding a hat or bonnet, altering the position of an arm or leg, increasing the depth of his shadows, and in many other ways.

This plate is $14\frac{6}{10}$ inches by $10\frac{1}{10}$ inches.

CHRIST HEALING THE SICK.

(THE HUNDRED GUILDER PIECE.)

ND Jesus went about all Galilee, teaching in their synagogues, and preaching the gospel of the kingdom, and healing all manner of sickness and all manner of disease among the people.   And his fame went throughout all Syria: and they brought unto him all sick people that were taken with divers diseases and torments, and those which were possessed with devils, and those which were lunatick, and those that had the palsy; and he healed them.—*Matthew* iv. 23, 24.

The piece known as the Hundred Guilder piece, represents our Lord healing the sick.

Christ is seen in front, standing a little to the left, with an extensive glory proceeding from his head.   He leans his left elbow upon some stone-work, and his left hand is held up; his right hand is stretched out towards the people, to whom he is speaking.   In front, towards the middle, a woman appears on a mattress, lying on the ground, depressed with languor and disease; above her, an old woman raises her shrivelled arms in a supplicating posture; another approaches our Saviour, carrying a child; these, with many other sick persons, implore his assistance.   To the left are many figures that appear to be spectators of the miracles; some of them seem to be disputing about the power or authority by which they are performed.   To the right are a great number of sick persons.   One in a wheelbarrow, with two figures just above him, an old woman leading an old man, are most admirably expressive of great age and decrepitude.   To the right of them an Æthiopian is seen, with a camel in the background, denoting that the fame of our Saviour's miracles had spread far abroad.   This piece is shadowed to the right, and on the left is illuminated.   It is generally esteemed the *chef-d'œuvre* of Rembrandt, being highly finished, the characters full of expression, and the effect of the *chiar'-oscuro* very fine.—*Daulby, No. 75.*

This etching, which is considered to be Rembrandt's masterpiece, has always been sought by amateurs with the greatest avidity.   It is said that Rembrandt would never sell an impression for less than one hundred guilders (about eight guineas).   At Mr. Esdaile's sale, in 1840, a proof of the first state of the plate, with the neck of the ass white, was bought by Messrs. Colnaghi for £231 !

In the second state, with the ass's neck etched upon, there is a proof in the Museum of Amsterdam, on the back of which is written, " Given to me by my esteemed friend Rembrandt, in exchange for a proof of Marc Antonio's.   Z. P. Zoomer."

There are two other known states of this plate, which was bought by Capt. Baillie, who retouched it, and after selling proofs for five guineas, cut it into four pieces, and sold proofs from each separately.

This plate is 15-$\frac{3}{10}$ inches in length by 11 inches in height.

V.

THE GOOD SAMARITAN.

ND Jesus answering said, A certain man went down from Jerusalem to Jericho, and fell among thieves, which stripped him of his raiment, and wounded him, and departed, leaving him half dead. And by chance there came down a certain priest that way : and when he saw him, he passed by on the other side. And likewise a Levite, when he was at the place, came and looked on him, and passed by on the other side. But a certain Samaritan, as he journeyed, came where he was : and when he saw him, he had compassion on him, and went to him, and bound up his wounds, pouring in oil and wine, and set him on his own beast, and brought him to an inn, and took care of him. And on the morrow when he departed, he took out two pence, and gave them to the host, and said unto him, Take care of him : and whatsoever thou spendest more, when I come again, I will repay thee.—*Luke* x. 30-35.

In the front a horse is seen, standing in profile, which a lacquey holds by the bridle. On the other side of the horse appears a man who carries in his arms the wounded traveller, whom he has just taken from his horse. On the left is a flight of steps which lead to the door of the inn, where the good Samaritan is charging the host to take proper care of his guest. To the left, a man in a cap and feather looks through a window. To the right is a well, from which a woman is drawing water, and in the distance beyond it, are seen several public buildings, and beyond them, a rock. The introduction of a dog, towards the right corner, in an attitude in the true Dutch style, is an injury to the composition (considered as a piece of sacred history), which otherwise is very fine, and richly picturesque. This is one of the pieces that Rembrandt has finished with the greatest care, producing a wonderful effect, with a fine point, and light hand. In the middle of the margin, at the bottom, is written, *Rembrandt inventor et fecit*, 1633.—*Daulby*, No. 77.

There are four states of this plate. In the first the tail of the horse is white. A proof of this was sold at Paris, in 1853, for £84. The second state, in which the horse's tail is shaded, is more rare than the first: the margin is reduced. In the third state, the wall of the flight of steps is also shaded. In the fourth state only is there the name and date.

ECCE HOMO.

HEN Pilate therefore took Jesus, and scourged him. And the soldiers platted a crown of thorns, and put it on his head, and they put on him a purple robe, and said, Hail, King of the Jews! and they smote him with their hands. Pilate therefore went forth again, and saith unto them, Behold, I bring him forth to you, that ye may know that I find no fault in him. Then came Jesus forth, wearing the crown of thorns, and the purple robe. And Pilate saith unto them, Behold the man!*—*John* xix. 1-5.

This piece is the companion of the Descent from the Cross, which is nearly the same size. The disposition of this piece was an arduous task, as it consists of an incredible number of figures. Pilate is standing under a canopy to the right; his left arm is extended, and he appears to be speaking to the crowd of Jews that are before him; one of whom is kneeling, with the reed in his left hand. Our Lord is seen in front, standing, surrounded by the guards, and exposed to gratify the malice of the populace. His eyes are raised to heaven, his arms hang down, and his hands are manacled and joined together before him; on his head is the crown of thorns. His body is naked, except a slight covering thrown over the shoulders and tied over the breast, and a cloth tied round his waist. At the foot of the judgment seat appears a Jew, who stretches out his right hand towards the crowd that fills the lower part of the print, and seems desirous of appeasing the fury of the people; promising them that their demands shall be satisfied. The background is rich in architecture. This piece is very scarce, and is highly esteemed; there are many fine heads in it, and it is extremely well executed, producing a great effect. In the margin is written, *Rembrandt ft.* 1636.— *Daulby, No.* 83.

There are four different states of this plate. In the first, the group consisting of Pilate, four other figures, and the Jew who stretches his hand towards the people, does not exist. In the second, the face of the Jew immediately above the man who holds the reed, is not shaded. A proof of this state was sold in Paris, in 1859, for £56. In the third state the Jew's face is shaded.

This plate is $21\frac{6}{10}$ inches by $17\frac{6}{10}$ inches.

---

* In the Latin Vulgate, ECCE HOMO.

VII

THE DESCENT FROM THE CROSS.

ND now when the even was come, because it was the preparation, that is, the day before the sabbath, Joseph of Arimathea, an honourable counsellor, which also waited for the kingdom of God, came, and went in boldly unto Pilate, and craved the body of Jesus. And Pilate marvelled if he were already dead: and calling unto him the centurion, he asked him whether he had been any while dead. And when he knew it of the centurion, he gave the body to Joseph. And he bought fine linen, and took him down, and wrapped him in the linen, and laid him in a sepulchre which was hewn out of a rock, and rolled a stone unto the door of the sepulchre. And Mary Magdalene, and Mary the mother of Joses, beheld where he was laid.—*Mark* xv. 42-47.

The companion of the " Ecce Homo." The subject is illuminated by the rays of light that fall from the sky directly upon the group, which is busied in taking down the body of Jesus Christ from the cross. In the upper part of the print, a man stands upon a ladder, leaning over the transverse beam of the cross, and holding with his right hand a corner of the sheet in which the body is to be wrapped. There are two other ladders reared against the cross, with a man on each; one of whom is supporting our Saviour by his left arm, and the other by his right. Two men stand below and sustain the body, which they receive in the sheet, the effect of their hands under which is well expressed. On the left stands Joseph of Arimathea, seen in profile, richly habited; the two ends of his turban hang down behind, and his garment is embroidered, and turned up with fur; his hand is supported on a walking stick. In the right corner is St. John, with the Virgin and Mary Magdalene, spreading a rich fringed carpet on the ground, to receive the body. Beyond them are several spectators, who appear to be suitably affected by this mournful event. The city of Jerusalem occupies the background. In the margin, a little to the left, is written *Rembrandt f. cum pryvl*. 1633. This print is extremely well executed; the composition is grand, the heads full ·of character, and the effect, in a good impression, very fine.—*Daulby, No.* 84.

Rembrandt etched this subject twice. Of the first plate, which was spoiled, probably by overheating the varnish, only three impressions are known—one in the Cabinet des Estampes, at Paris, another in the British Museum, and the third in the Amsterdam Museum.

Of the second plate there are two states. In the first, the legs of the two men who receive the body of Christ are etched with single strokes. In the second state these legs are finished with cross hatchings, and in the margin is written *Rembrandt f. cum pryvlo*, 1633. On some impressions the names of engravers are added.

Rembrandt painted this composition, with some alterations in the effect. It is now in the Pinacotheca of Munich.

This plate is $20\frac{9}{10}$ inches high by $16\frac{1}{10}$ inches wide.

VIII

THE DEATH OF THE VIRGIN.

HE disposition of this subject is grand; it is executed in a masterly manner and produces a fine effect. The Virgin appears to be expiring in a bed, the curtains of which being drawn up, discover the posts, richly ornamented. Near it are many persons, several of them weeping. A physician feels her pulse with great attention, while Joseph raises up the pillow on which rests her head, and holds a handkerchief to her nose. To the left sits a Jewish Rabbi at a table, seen from behind, reading in a large book. Above the table, near the head of the bed, stands the high priest; his arms hang down, and his hands are clasped together before him; he looks with a fixed and mournful attention on the Virgin. At the side of the high priest is a boy holding a great crosier. At the foot of the bed stands a tall woman, with her hands raised and clasped together, and behind her, St. John, with his arms extended; both of them appear to be in great affliction. To the right is a large curtain, which a person from behind opens with his right hand; he has a turban on his head, and his face has some resemblance of Rembrandt's. In the right corner is an elbow chair. Above the bed, surrounded with a luminous glory, is seen an angel, with several cherubs, the faces of which are all ill expressed. To the left, at the bottom, is written *Rembrandt f.* 1639.— *Daulby, No.* 97.

There are three states of this plate. In the first, the top of the elbow chair which stands in the corner is indicated by a single stroke. In the second, it is shaded, and the back of the chair is more worked upon. In the third state the plate, which is still in existence, has been entirely retouched.

This plate is 16 inches high by $12\frac{8}{10}$ inches wide.

IX

SAINT JEROME.

(*Unfinished*).

T is much to be regretted that the whole of this plate was not finished. The disposition of the subject is rich, and that part which is done is in good style. The composition is much in the manner of Albert Dürer. St. Jerome is sitting on a bank or rock to the left, at the foot of a large tree, the higher part of what is seen of it being unfinished; on the trunk, a bird is perched. There is a clump of trees immediately behind it in shade. The figure of St. Jerome is only traced with the outline, except the hat and upper part of the face, which are nearly finished. The bank on which he sits, which takes up almost the foreground of the print, is likewise only traced. He rests upon his left elbow, and holds a book in both hands, in which he is reading. On the bank behind him stands a lion, in a spirited attitude, seen from behind ; his hinder part is only etched with the single stroke. In the distance, to the right, is a country house and a church, with clumps of trees on each side of them, which are all well finished. Beneath the church is a fall of water, which tumbles down, amongst the rocks, to the right corner of the print. Over the water-fall is a wooden bridge, with two figures at the end of it.—*Daulby, No.* 104.

In the first impressions of this plate the piles of the bridge are but slightly indicated ; in the second state they are much more shaded.

X

HAMAN AND MORDECAI.

ND Haman answered the king, For the man whom the king delighteth to honour, let the royal apparel be brought which the king useth to wear, and the horse that the king rideth upon, and the crown royal which is set upon his head: and let this apparel and horse be delivered to the hand of one of the king's most noble princes, that they may array the man withal whom the king delighteth to honour, and bring him on horseback through the street of the city, and proclaim before him, Thus shall it be done to the man whom the king delighteth to honour. Then the king said to Haman, Make haste, and take the apparel and the horse, as thou hast said, and do even so to Mordecai the Jew, that sitteth at the king's gate: let nothing fail of all that thou hast spoken. Then took Haman the apparel and the horse, and arrayed Mordecai, and brought him on horseback through the street of the city, and proclaimed before him, Thus shall it be done unto the man whom the king delighteth to honour.—*Esther* vi. 7-1.1

Mordecai, mounted on the king's horse, and arrayed in royal apparel, with a sceptre in his right hand, is conducted in triumph by Haman in the midst of the people. He is at the king's gate, through which, at a distance, is seen a round temple. Haman, who appears in front, extends his arms, and seems to proclaim, " Thus shall it be done to the man whom the king delighteth to honour." To the right, king Ahasuerus, with his queen Esther, are looking out of the palace. A concourse of people attend, who appear affected with respect and admiration. This piece is executed in a good style, and is full of work. It is esteemed one of Rembrandt's most beautiful prints.—*Daulby, No.* 39.

There are two states of this plate. In the second, which is much worn, the beard of Mordecai has been retouched by an unskilful hand.

XI

DOCTOR FAUSTUS.

THE Doctor is standing in his laboratory, on the left side, behind a table, on which he rests his right hand; and his left rests on an arm of his chair. His face is in profile, he has a white cap on his head, and he is looking with a fixed attention on some magic characters which he sees in a mirror held out by a figure, of which only the hands are discovered. These characters are placed in the middle of a casement. At the right corner, at the bottom, is a globe, of which only half is discovered. Behind him part of a curtain is seen, drawn on a rod, and near it a skull. By all which it appears that he was supposed to be an adept in the mysteries of the Cabbala. This piece is highly finished, and the *chiar'-oscuro* has a wonderful effect.—*Daulby, No.* 250.

M. Charles Blanc has discovered three states of this plate. Proofs of the first state are generally upon India paper, and are very rare. In the second state, there is more etching on the shoulder of the figure; and in the third, the ray of light is divided by additional lines.

XII

THE RAT-KILLER.

THIS piece represents an old man, holding in his left hand a pole, with a cage on the top of it containing rats. On the top of the cage sits a live one, and from the bottom is suspended a dead one; there is likewise a rat perched on his shoulder. He has a high cap on, and a sword hanging by his side, with a short fur cloak thrown over his right arm, and hanging behind him. He is accompanied by a little boy, who carries a box of ratsbane; the old man offers a packet of it to another, who is leaning over a door-hatch to the left; he puts it aside with his hand, rejecting it, and likewise turns his head from it. By the side of the door appear the trunk of an old blasted tree, and a broken cart. To the right, in the distance, is a cottage, with trees appearing above it. Near the bottom, on the right side, is written, *Rt.* 1632, the 3, with the 2 after it, are reversed.—*Daulby, No.* 117.

There are two states of this plate. In the first impressions, which are very scarce, the trees above the head of the rat-killer are not cross-etched.

XIII

VIEW OF OMVAL, NEAR AMSTERDAM.

HIS subject is well chosen, and finely executed. On the foreground to the left is a clump of trees; one of them is the venerable trunk of a large tree which appears to be nearly dead. On a bank, amongst these trees, a young couple are sitting. The youth is putting a garland on the head of the young woman. To the right of the trees, stands a peasant seen from behind, looking at a covered barge, full of people, sailing on the river. Over the river is seen the village of Omval; before it lie several boats, and to the right are two windmills. At the right corner, at the bottom, is written *Rembrant*, 1645, the *d* being omitted. It is scarce.—*Daulby, No.* 201.

XIV

A VIEW OF AMSTERDAM.

THIS piece is executed in a good style, with a very fine point. The foreground is a marsh. The river Amstel crosses the print; beyond it, Amsterdam is seen in a point of view which exhibits many churches; and to the right several windmills. In the centre a large double-roofed building, with a windmill near it, particularly attract the eye. To the left lies the shipping. This piece is scarce.—*Daulby, No.* 202.

Ordinary impressions from this plate are frequently to be met with.

XV

THE THREE TREES.

HIS is a very fine landscape; known by this name, because to the right, on an eminence, is a singular group of three trees, through which, on a rising ground, is perceived a waggon, full of peasants, part of which is intercepted by the trunk of the right-hand tree, and some houses are likewise intercepted by the trunk of the middle tree. In the left front is a large piece of water; on the other side of it, on a bank, stands a man who is angling; a woman is sitting near him. In the distance is a large town, with several churches in it, and between the piece of water and the town are several groups of cattle and figures. The sky is covered with dark clouds, and a shower of rain is falling to the left. Beneath some water-weeds on the left, near the bottom, is written *Rembrandt f.* 1643. This piece is esteemed the best and most finished of all the landscapes of Rembrandt; it is executed in a good style, and produces a great effect. —*Daulby, No.* 204.

Good proofs of this plate are rare. They are distinguished by the burr upon the work in the sky, which is chiefly executed with dry-point.

In an impression in the Amsterdam Museum, M. Charles Blanc has traced the scarcely visible outline form of a giant, who, it may be supposed, is the Spirit of the Storm. The figure is in the dim part of the sky above the trees.

XVI

A LARGE LANDSCAPE WITH A MILL SAIL SEEN

ABOVE A COTTAGE.

N the left are two large trees; but the boundary of the plate does not admit of their being carried up above half their proper height. Behind the spreading one is a large thatched cottage, above which appears the sail of a mill. The door of the cottage is open, and a boy is standing within it, with a younger child in a stooping posture before him. In front of the cottage a wooden platform projects into a canal or river, that runs nearly across the print, and, meandering, loses itself in the distance on the right, which is terminated with a view of a village, in which a tower-steeple and a windmill are conspicuous objects. To the right, on a bank near some water weeds, is a duck pluming itself, and another on the water is swimming towards it On the bank is written *Rembrandt f.* 1641. This piece is not common.—*Daulby, No.* 222.

CORNELIUS ANSLO..

NSLO was an Anabaptist minister. He is represented sitting in an elbow-chair behind a covered table, on the middle of which is an inkstand; he holds a pen in his right hand, which is supported on a book that stands upright, and with his left he points to another lying open, which rests against two more, one lying on the other. His beard is dark and bushy; he has on a gown turned up with fur, a ruff round his neck, and a broad-brimmed hat. The background is shaded with the double stroke, nearly as high as the top of the chair on the left, and is lightly touched in many places, to give it the character of an inner wall; on the right is a nail driven into it. On the back of a chair, above the three books, is written *Rembrandt f.* 1641, but the figure 4 is reversed. This is one of Rembrandt's best portraits, and is very scarce; it is highly finished, and produces a fine effect.—*Daulby, No.* 251.

This portrait was wrongly named by Gersaint, who confounded Renier Hanslo, the poet, with the celebrated preacher, Cornelius Anslo.

There are two states of this plate. In the first, which is very rare, there is a white margin at the bottom of the plate, which is covered with etching in the second state.

There is a copy extant of this portrait, so faithfully made, that the most experienced critics are deceived by it.

XVIII.

CLEMENT DE JONGE.

HIS is the portrait of a printseller; he is represented a half-length in front, sitting in an elbow chair; his hair is short and straight, he has a broad-brimmed hat on, turned up at the sides, and wears a cloak which is open before, and he has gloves on; his right arm rests on the elbow of the chair, which raises the hand opposite to his breast, the other falling on his left knee. The background is etched on the left side, as high as the hat, and on the right, as high as the elbow. In the right corner, at the bottom, in all the impressions, is written *Rembrandt f.* 1651.—*Daulby, No. 252.*

There are six states of this plate. In the first, which is extremely rare, there is a small space unetched on the back of the chair. The shadow beneath the hat, on the right side, is one uniform grey, and there is an angular patch of white beneath the right eye. In the second state, the shadow and the white spaces have been etched on. In the third, the form of the hat has been altered; and the fourth and fifth present some slight further variations. The sixth has been retouched by an unskilful hand; a patch of black being formed on the right shoulder, and the expression of the eyes altered.

XIX

YOUNG HAARING.

E was the son of the Burgomaster, Jacob Haaring. This piece is executed in Rembrandt's dark manner, and the *chiar'-oscuro* has a strong effect. The light comes through the window, and falls full on his left cheek and band, and the rest of the subject is kept down in shade. He is sitting in an elbow chair, rather inclining towards the left; he rests both hands on the arms of the chair, and holds his hat in his right hand. There is a curtain rod that crosses the window, about one third from the top of it, and the curtain is drawn to the right side. On the lower row of the window panes is written, *Rembrandt f.* 1655, the 6 is reversed.—*Daulby, No.* 255.

This portrait is called Young Haaring, to distinguish it from that of his father, whom also Rembrandt etched. The son's name was Thomas; he was " concierge" of the Insolvent Court at Amsterdam, and in this capacity, about a year after this etching was finished, had to superintend the sale of Rembrandt's house and furniture.

There are five states of this plate. In the first, which is very rare, there is no curtain rod nor curtain. In the second state, there is a rod across the window, and a curtain hanging from it. In the third, a little picture is added at the bottom. In the fourth state, this picture is effaced; and in the fifth, the plate is considerably cut down.

XX.

JOHN LUTMA.

HIS person was a noted goldsmith of Groningen. His portrait is one of Rembrandt's best; the expression in the face is particularly spirited. He is sitting in an elbow chair, with his arms resting upon it, and holds something like a metal figure in his right hand; he has on a black velvet cap; his hair is very short, and his beard bushy. At his left elbow is a table, on which lies a scollop, with a box of gravers and a hammer. On the top corners of the chair are two grotesque heads. Above the table is written (but apparently not by Rembrandt) *Joannes Lutma, aurifex natus Groningæ.* To the right is a window, and in the right corner of it stands a water bottle. In the top left corner of the window is written *Rembrandt f.* 1656.—*Daulby, No.* 256.

There are three different states of this plate. In the first, there is no window, neither are there any names or date. In the second, the window and the writing have been added. In the third, the height of the picture is reduced, there being no margin at the bottom. This state is much inferior to the others, and its great rarity constitutes its chief value.

XXI.

EPHRAIM BONUS.

(LE JUIF À LA RAMPE.)

HIS person was a Jewish physician. He is represented coming down a staircase, with his right hand on the balustrade; his head is seen nearly in front, with a high crowned hat on; his hair is short and dark, and he has a Jewish beard; a short cloak covers his left shoulder, under which the hand and arm are concealed, and on the forefinger of his right hand is a diamond ring. He has a band round his neck, and a cuff at his sleeve. This piece is one of Rembrandt's finest portraits; the face is full of expression, and the *chiar'-oscuro* has a masterly effect. Towards the bottom, at the right corner, is to be read (though with difficulty), *Rembrandt f.* 1647.—*Daulby, No.* 258.

Ephraim Bonus was a Portuguese by birth, and settled in Amsterdam in the first half of the seventeenth century. In 1651 he was made a Burgomaster. Speaking of this etching, one writer has observed,—" He appears as if deliberating on the case of a patient," and as if doubtful whether he will not remount the stairs.

This is perhaps the most famous of all Rembrandt's portraits. There are but three proofs known of the first state of the plate. These are called " with the black ring"— because in these early impressions the burr on the plate caused the ring to print quite black. One is in the Amsterdam Museum; one, which cost £138, and from which the photograph is taken, in the British Museum; and the third in the Collection of Mr. Holford.

In the second state of the plate the ring is white, and the hand and the balusters of the stairs are more worked upon.

XXII.

UYTENBOGAERT, A DUTCH MINISTER.

HIS minister was of the sect of the Remonstrants, and lived under the govern-
ment of Prince Maurice, whom he always opposed, and for some time
successfully; but was at length obliged to fly from the Prince's resentment. This
portrait is executed in an oval, squared at the bottom, in an irregular octagon plate. He
is sitting at a table in a gown faced with fur; he wears the calotte cap, and has a ruff
round his neck. His hair is short, and appears to be turned grey, the beard is likewise
short and thick; his face is nearly a full front, with the body turned a little to the right;
his right hand is supported on the arm of the chair; in his left hand is a book open,
which rests upon some others lying on the table, and farther back are several other
books thrown negligently one upon another. Behind him is a pillar, and to the right of it,
an arch in the background. On each side of the print, a curtain is drawn aside. This
is a fine portrait, highly finished, and produces a strong effect. In the two angles at
the top is written, *Rembrandt f.* 1635. It is scarce. Under the print are the following
Latin verses, by Grotius :

> " Quem pia mirari plebes, quem castra solebant,
>   Damnare et mores aula coacta suos,
>   Jactatus multum, nec tantum fractus ab annis
>   WTENDOGARDUS sic tutus, Haga redit."—II. GROTIUS.

Daulby, No. 259.

John Uytenbogaert, who was born at Utrecht in 1557, was a man of considerable
eminence, and took a prominent part in the religious controversies which agitated Holland
in the early part of the seventeenth century. For fifteen years he was chaplain to the
Prince of Orange, whom he followed in all his campaigns. He was a friend of Arminius,
and was obliged to take refuge at Amiens, Paris, and Rouen. In 1625 Uytenbogaert
returned to Amsterdam, where he continued to reside until he died in the year 1644.

There are four states of this plate. In the first, a proof of which is in the Amsterdam
Museum, there is no curtain, nor the Latin verses; and the ruff round the neck is only
sketched out. In the second the ruff is more worked upon. In the third the curtain is
added, and the character of the head is altered. The plate is reduced to an octagon
form, but with " ears" at the right and left extremities. In the fourth state, which is
common, the plate is an octagon without the ears.

XXIII

JOHN CORNELIUS SYLVIUS.

YLVIUS was a minister of great learning. This portrait is an oval, round which is written, *Spes mea Christus,* which was his motto, and *Johannes Cornelii Sylvius. Amstelodamo:* with other inscriptions in Latin, and under the portrait are Latin verses by C. Barleus. This is esteemed one of Rembrandt's best portraits. It is very scarce, especially if a good impression; the etching is so tender that many could not be taken off before the plate was worn. The head, which is nearly a full front, is finely executed; it is covered with a calotte, the hair and beard are white; the hair is short, but the beard is long, divided in the middle, and pointed; round the neck is a ruff; his gown is faced with fur at the breast, and at the sleeves, which are short and open. The fingers of his left hand are placed in a book, which is closed, and lies on a desk before him. He stoops a little, and is addressing his audience with his right hand, which projects in front, and casts a shadow that extends beyond the oval; as likewise does the book, and the effect thereby produced is very singular and striking. Behind him is a pillar, and on the left side, a curtain, which is drawn up, and which likewise casts some little shade beyond the oval. A square is described without the oval. On the pillar, near the top, is written, *Rembrandt* 1646.—*Daulby, No.* 260.

M. Le Blanc states that the portrait known as that of Janius Sylvius represents the same person at a somewhat earlier period of his life. It is dated 1633. In delicacy of execution and general excellence as a work of art it is not equal to the later portrait.

Sylvius was connected with Rembrandt by marriage, his wife being a cousin of Saskia Uilenburg, Rembrandt's first wife. The very few early impressions from this plate may be recognized by the velvet-like appearance of the beard, and the colour of the lower part of the proof, particularly in the corners.

XXIV

UYTENBOGAERT, THE BANKER.

HIS is likewise one of the finest and scarcest portraits in the collection. The composition, effect, and execution, are all in the best style. In Holland it is called the "Goldweigher," and in France, the "Banker." Uytenbogaert was Receiver General to the States of Holland. He is represented sitting in the counting-house. His face is seen nearly in front, with moustaches; his hair is short; he has on a velvet cap. His head inclines a little over his right shoulder, which gives great spirit to the attitude. His gown is turned up before, and at the sleeves, with fur. He holds a pen in his right hand, which rests on a large account-book, that lies open on a desk standing on a table covered with a richly flowered cloth, fringed at the bottom, on which are several bags of money. He is delivering a bag to a man, who is kneeling on his left knee, and appears to be receiving it in order to pack it in a cask that stands before him with the head off. Two other casks lie on their sides, with a mallet and driver lying upon one of them. On the left side is a large iron chest. Over the table is a shelf suspended from the ceiling, on which lie several bundles of papers; and from it hangs a pair of scales, in one of which is a bag of money. In the background, on the left, stand two persons behind a door-hatch, as if waiting to transact business. On the wall is a large arched picture, which represents the history of the Brazen Serpent; to the right of it hangs a sword. In the margin is written, *Rembrandt f.* 1639.—*Daulby, No.* 261.

There is but little known concerning the original of this portrait. His name occurs more than once in the correspondence between Rembrandt and Constantine Huygens, the secretary of Prince Frederick Henri, regarding the sums to be paid for certain pictures; and doubtless it was from having to go to the banker to receive money that Rembrandt became acquainted with him.

There are three states of this plate. In the first, which is extremely rare, the head of the banker is simply outlined. In the second state, which is very rare, the head is finished. In the third, the plate has been retouched all over, and very much spoiled. Impressions from this state are usually upon thick and coarse India paper.

XXV

VAN COPPENOL, THE WRITING-MASTER.

HIS portrait is esteemed a capital piece of this master; the countenance is very expressive, and the whole is highly finished. He is sitting before a table turned to the right, but his face is nearly a full front; his head is covered with the calotte, his hair short and white, with small moustaches, but no beard. He has a large, plain band round his neck; his habit is a kind of cassock, with very small buttons near together, and with open cuffs at his sleeves. Over the cassock is a gown, or cloak, open, and falling back with a tassel at the cape. He holds a blank paper with both hands, and in his right hand is a pen. The plate was probably damaged, for it was cut to a size which takes in little more than the head, measuring (including a margin of half an inch) 6 by $5\frac{2}{10}$. This reduced plate is still in existence in France, and there are good impressions of it, which shows that there were not many taken off when entire, for the head is delicately etched. Coppenol wrote some verses under the entire print, as likewise under the smaller portraits of himself. They are curiously written, and enhance the value of those impressions on which they are found.—*Daulby, No.* 263.

Of this plate five states are known. In the first, the background is white, with the exception of a column on the left. This column is shaded with a single stroke to half its height. The right sleeve is white. Of this state only two examples exist.

In the second state the background is white, but the column is shaded nearly to the top, and the sleeve is shaded with a single stroke.

In the third state a curtain is substituted for the column, and there is more work on the coat, especially on the left sleeve. In the fourth, the folds of the curtain are more defined, and there is additional work on the sleeves.

In the fifth, the plate has been cut down, so that only the head and shoulders of the figure remain.

XXVI

THE BURGOMASTER SIX.

HIS celebrated portrait and that of Van Tol, are the most valuable in this class. An impression of Van Tol has been sold for fifty guineas, and the same sum has been given for a first impression of this portrait. It must indeed be confessed that, besides its rarity, it is one of Rembrandt's best performances; the *chiar'-oscuro* is as finely preserved as in his best paintings. The Burgomaster is represented a full-length, standing, and leaning his back against a window, the lower casement of which is open. He is reading a quarto pamphlet, which he holds doubled in his hands. As the whole piece is illuminated from the window, all the light that is thrown upon the face is by reflection from the book. The manner in which Rembrandt has expressed the attention of his friend and patron to the subject he is reading is inimitable. His hair is full and bushy, waving gently and gracefully to his shoulders; his habit and neck-band are open before, with tassels hanging down, and his cloak is thrown off behind him, part of it lying on the window frame, and part on a table, on which lie his sword and belt. His cane stands on the table, leaning against the wall, and over it hangs his hat, with a short sword near the top of the cane. Above the table is an historical picture, with a curtain drawn before part of it. In the left corner, in front, stands a chair, with a cushion and three books on it, the uppermost of which is open. On the right side of the window a curtain is drawn back in a festoon. Beneath the window the floor is raised a step, and the wall is covered with matting, which Gersaint mistakes for stone-work. In a narrow margin of an eighth of an inch is written, to the right, *Rembrandt f.* 1647, and on the left, *Jan Six Æ,* and a little farther on, 29.—*Daulby, No.* 265.

Of this plate three states are known. In the first, there is seen at the window a stone shelf behind the burgomaster; the names of Rembrandt and Six do not yet appear. The Museum at Amsterdam and the Cabinet des Estampes at Paris each possess a copy of this state. In the second, the stone shelf has been removed; the name of Rembrandt is engraved with the date 1647; the figures 6 and 4 are reversed. Impressions of this state are rare, and are as fine as the first, especially when printed on India paper. In the third state *Jan Six Æ* 29 has been added, and the figures 6 and 4 have been re-engraved in the ordinary position. Impressions of this state exist, which are vigorous and delicate, but they are very rare.

Six, in addition to his love of art, possessed considerable literary talent. He was the author of several poems and other works. He died in 1700, at the age of 82.

At Mr. Thorel's sale in Paris, in 1853, an impression from the second state of this plate was sold for £140; and in March, 1861, at the sale of M. Ferol, a superb proof of the same state fetched the enormous sum of £250.

XXVII

PORTRAIT OF REMBRANDT DRAWING.

N this portrait Rembrandt has laid aside the superb cap and feather, and repre-sented himself as a complete Dutch character. This print is finely etched, and highly finished in his dark manner. It is a full-front, half-length. His head is covered with a narrow-brimmed hat, his garment is very plain, and open at the neck. He is sitting at a table, which is in the front of the print, and holds a crayon in his right hand, with which he is drawing on paper, placed upon a book, on which he rests his left. Upon the left side is a casement open, through which a landscape is seen at a distance. Of this piece the strongest impressions are the best, the strokes of the plate being extremely light and tender. On a short curtain or screen, hanging from the top of the casement, is written *Rembrandt f.* 1648.—*Daulby, No.* 27.

Of this, which is one of the finest portraits of Rembrandt, no less than ten states have been described, but of the first two no examples can now be traced in any collections, either public or private.

The first is mentioned by Claussin as being only an outline; Wilson refers to a second, rather more finished. In the third, the face, previously pale and without force, is life-like and effective; the figure is highly finished, but the hands and wristbands are white. In the fourth state the upper part of the left side of the plate has been made regular in outline, which it was not in the earlier impressions; there is further work on the plate, but the hands and wristbands are still white. In the fifth, the name of Rembrandt and the date 1648 have been added on a scroll at the top of the window. In the sixth, the left hand is lightly shaded. In the seventh, the right hand is similarly shaded, and there are some additional fine strokes on the face, especially on the left temple. The eighth is very similar, but there are some fine vertical lines on the right side of the paper, and the wristband of the left hand is worked with a light stroke. In the ninth, a landscape is seen through the window, and there are additional light touches on other parts of the plate. In the tenth, the plate has been heavily retouched, and with the worst possible effect; the shadow beneath the right hand is overcharged with ink; the name of Rembrandt on the scroll is no longer visible.

In addition to these are modern impressions taken from the plate in its present very deteriorated condition; but there is no probability of such prints being in the possession of a connoisseur.

XXVIII

THE GREAT JEWISH BRIDE.

HIS is a fine portrait, highly finished. The bride is sitting in an elbow chair, her face is a three-quarters, turned to the left; her hair is long, flowing over her shoulders down to her waist; her head, round which is a string of pearls, is uncovered, according to the custom in Holland among the Jewish women when they go to be married; she rests her right hand on the end of the elbow of the chair in which she is sitting, and in her left she holds a scroll of paper. She has a kind of toilet gown over her other apparel. Close by her right hand is a table, on which lie several bundles of papers and books. The background consists of stonework; on the left side is an arch. On the cloth which covers the table is the letter *R* reversed.—*Daulby, No.* 311.

M. Le Blanc asserts that this portrait is erroneously named, and that, in reality, it represents the first wife of Rembrandt. The reasons he advances in support of his opinion are numerous, and it is at least extremely probable that he is correct in his judgment.

There are four states known of this plate. The first is very rare; in it the bust only of the figure is finished, and the background is less worked on than in the subsequent states. In the second state, which is even more scarce, the background is rather more finished. The third presents vertical mouldings in the stonework of the background. In the fourth, the hands and the toilet gown, which are white in the earlier impressions, are covered with light strokes.

XXIX

REMBRANDT'S MOTHER.

HE is turned a little to the right, her eyes look downward; her head is covered with a black, open veil: her habit is black, and her left hand is placed high up on her breast. The face is finely finished with a light point, and is very expressive of old age; the background is shaded. In the margin, towards the left, is written, *Rt.* 1631.—*Daulby, No.* 318.

There appears to be only one state of this plate. Wilson mentions an earlier state in which the background is less worked on, especially around the head; but more recent authorities do not confirm his opinion.

XXX.

A PORTRAIT OF REMBRANDT, WITH A DRAWN SABRE.

(Frontispiece).

THIS piece is extremely well executed. He is seen full-face, with a richly ornamented cap, his hair is full and frizzled, and he has moustaches. In his right
hand he holds a glittering sabre. His habit is embroidered, and the top enriched with
ermine and a string of jewels. The background is shaded on the left as high as the
shoulder. At the top, on the left, is written *Rembrandt f.* 1634.—*Daulby, No.* 23.

This is the most celebrated of the many portraits which Rembrandt executed of
himself, not only because of its great excellence, but because of the rarity of the proofs
in the first state of the plate, of which only four are known to exist. One in the
Museum at Amsterdam, a second in the possession of Lord Aylesford, who paid 350
guineas for it, a third in the print room of the Bibliothèque, in Paris, and the fourth,
which formerly belonged to Jean Pierre Zoomer, of Amsterdam, a contemporary and
friend of Rembrandt's, was bought at M. Verstolk's sale, in 1847, for the British Museum,
at the price of 150 guineas. It is from this impression that the photograph is taken.

There are two other states of this plate. In the second state, impressions of which
are rare, the plate is cut into an oval-shaped octagon; and in the third state it is a
perfect oval.

APPENDIX.

A CATALOGUE OF REMBRANDT'S ETCHINGS.

Compiled by Daniel Daulby, from the Catalogues of De Burgy, Gersaint,
Helle and Glomy, Marcus, and Yver, and now used in the
Print Room of the British Museum.

I. Portraits of Rembrandt, or Heads which resemble Him.

 HE Portrait of Rembrandt drawing.
2. The Bust of a Young Man resembling Rembrandt.
3. A Head very much resembling Rembrandt, well etched, and highly finished.
4. Another Portrait of Rembrandt, called the Bird of Prey portrait.
5. A Bust of a Young Man resembling Rembrandt.
6. A Small Head, stooping, somewhat resembling Rembrandt.
7. A Bust of a Young Man, resembling Rembrandt, coarsely etched.
8. A Portrait of Rembrandt whilst he was young.
9. A Head resembling Rembrandt.
10. A Head of Rembrandt, in a cap, which is more highly finished than the portrait.
11. A Portrait resembling Rembrandt, highly etched on a narrow plate, and unfinished.
12. A Portrait of Rembrandt, etched in the early part of his life.
13. A Bust of a Young Man, resembling Rembrandt.
14. A Bust, in which there is some resemblance of Rembrandt in his youth.
15. A Portrait of Rembrandt when young.
16. A Bust of Titus, Son of Rembrandt.
17. A small Portrait of Rembrandt in a cap and fur cloak.
18. A Bust of a Young Man resembling Rembrandt.
19. A Bust which resembles Rembrandt in his youth.
20. A Bust resembling Rembrandt.

21. A Bust very much resembling Rembrandt.
22. A Portrait of Rembrandt.
23. A Portrait of Rembrandt, with a drawn sabre.
24. The Portrait of Rembrandt and his Wife.
25. A Portrait of Rembrandt in the Mezetin cap and feather.
26. A fine Portrait of Rembrandt.
27. The Portrait of Rembrandt drawing.
28. A Portrait of Rembrandt in an oval.

II. Scripture Subjects from the Old Testament.

29. Adam and Eve.
30. Abraham entertaining the Three Angels.
31. Abraham sending away Hagar and Ishmael.
32. Abraham with his son Isaac.
33. Abraham's Sacrifice.
34. Four Prints for a Spanish Book—
    Jacob's Ladder.
    The Combat of David with Goliath.
    The Image which Nebuchadnezzar saw in his dream.
    The Vision of Ezekiel.
35. Jacob lamenting the supposed death of Joseph.
36. Joseph and Potiphar's Wife.
37. Joseph telling his dream to his Brethren in the presence of his Father and Mother.
38. Gideon's sacrifice.
39. Haman and Mordecai.
40. David on his knees.
41. Tobit.
42. The Angel ascending from Tobit and his family.

III. Scripture Subjects from the New Testament.

43. The Angel appearing to the Shepherds.
44. The Nativity, or Adoration of the Shepherds.
45. The Nativity, a night piece.
46. The Circumcision.

47. The Little Circumcision.
48. The Circumcision. (Berendreck *ex.*)
49. The Presentation of Jesus in the Vaulted Temple.
50. The Presentation, in Rembrandt's dark manner.
51. The Presentation, with the Angel.
52. The Little Flight into Egypt.
53. The Flight into Egypt, a night piece.
54. The Return from Egypt.
55. The Flight into Egypt, the Holy Family crossing a rill.
56. The Flight into Egypt, in the style of Elsheimer.
57. The Rest in Egypt, in a wood, by night.
58. Three Pieces which are generally classed together; the Rest in Egypt, St. Peter, and a Man with a Pen.
59. The Rest in Egypt, (*unique.*)
60. The Virgin and the Infant Jesus in the clouds.
61. The Holy Family.
62. The Holy Family, Joseph looking in at the window.
63. Jesus disputing with the Doctors in the Temple, a sketch.
64. The same subject, a larger sketch.
65. The same subject, a small upright.
66. Little La Tombe.
67. The Tribute to Cæsar.
68. Christ delivering the Keys to St. Peter.
69. Jesus Christ driving the Money-changers out of the Temple.
70. The Prodigal Son.
71. Jesus and the Samaritan Woman at the Well,—arched.
72. Jesus and the Samaritan Woman at the Well,—an upright.
73. The Small Resurrection of Lazarus.
74. The Larger Resurrection of Lazarus.
75. The Hundred Guilder Piece.
76. Jesus Christ healing the Sick.
77. The Good Samaritan.
78. Our Lord in the Garden of Olives.
79. Our Lord before Pilate.
80. The Three Crosses.
81. Our Lord on the Cross between the Two Thieves, an oval.

82. The Little Crucifixion.
83. The Ecce Homo.
84. The Descent from the Cross.
85. The Descent from the Cross, a sketch.
86. The Descent from the Cross, a night piece.
87. Jesus Christ entombed.
88. The Funeral of Jesus.
89. The Virgin mourning the Death of Jesus.
90. Our Lord and his Disciples at Emmaus.
91. Our Lord and the Disciples at Emmaus, the little print.
92. The Decollation of St. John the Baptist.
93. The Decollation of St. John, doubtful.
94. St. Peter and St. John at the Beautiful Gate of the Temple.
95. The Baptism of the Eunuch.
96. The Angel delivering Saint Peter out of Prison.
97. The Death of the Virgin.
98. The Martyrdom of Saint Stephen.

IV. Pious Subjects.

99. Saint Jerome, unique.
100. Saint Jerome sitting at the foot of a tree.
101. Saint Jerome kneeling, arched.
102. Saint Jerome before the trunk of an old tree.
103. Saint Jerome kneeling.
104. Saint Jerome, unfinished.
105. Saint Jerome.
106. Saint Jerome, in Rembrandt's dark manner.
107. Saint Francis praying.
108. The Hour of Death.
109. Youth surprised by Death.
110 A Man meditating.

V. Fancy Pieces.

111. An Allegorical Piece.
112. The Star of the Kings.

113. Four Hunting Pieces.
114. Three Oriental Figures.
115. The Blind Beggar.
116. The Spanish Gipsy.
117. The Rat Killer.
118. The Rat Killer (*presque-unique*).
119. The Goldsmith.
120. The Pancake Woman.
121. The Sport of Kolef.
122. A Jews' Synagogue.
123. Fortune, an allegorical piece.
124. The Marriage of Jason and Creusa.
125. The Corn Cutter.
126. The Schoolmaster.
127. The Mountebank.
128. The Draughtsman.
129. Peasants travelling.
130. Cupid reposing.
131. The Jew with the high cap.
132. An Old Man with a boy.
133. The Onion Woman.
134. The Peasant with his hands behind him.
135. A Man playing at cards.
136. The Old Man with a short beard and a stick.
137. The Blind Fiddler.
138. The Man on Horseback.
139. The Polander.
140. Another Polander.
141. An Old Man seen from behind.
142. The Two Travelling Peasants.
143. The Old Man without a beard.
144. The Old Man with a bushy beard.
145. The Persian.
146. A Blind Man.
147. The Astrologer.
148. The Two Venetian Figures.

149. A Little Polish Figure.
150. A Physician feeling the pulse of his patient.
151. The Skater.
152. The Hog.
153. The Little Dog sleeping.
154. The Shell.

VI. BEGGARS.

155. A Beggar standing, spiritedly etched.
156. A Beggar, a profile in a cap.
157. Two Beggars, a man and a woman conversing.
158. Two other Beggars coming from behind a bank.
159. A Beggar, in the manner of Callot.
160. A Beggar in a slashed cloak.
161. A Beggar Woman, in Callot's manner.
162. A Beggar standing.
163. A Beggar with his dog in a string, arched.
164. A Beggar Woman asking alms.
165. Lazarus Klap, or the Dumb Beggar.
166. The Ragged Mariner, with his hands behind him.
167. A Beggar warming his hands over a chafingdish.
168. A Beggar with his mouth open.
169. An Old Beggar with a long beard, and a dog by his side.
170. Beggars at the door of a house.
171. A Beggar, and its companion, in two pieces.
172. A Beggar with a wooden leg.
173. A Peasant standing with his hands behind him, and a basket at his feet.
174. A Beggar, a sketch, unique.
175. Two Beggars, a man and a woman, presque-unique.
176. A Beggar, in Callot's manner, unique.
177. A Sick Beggar lying on the ground.

VII. FREE SUBJECTS.

178. Ledikant; the French Bed.
179. The Friar in the Straw.

180. The Flute Player.
181. The Shepherds in the Wood.
182. A Man with a bundle at his back.
183. A Woman crouching under a tree.

VIII. ACADEMICAL SUBJECTS.

184. A Painter drawing, after a model.
185. An Academical figure of a man, called in Holland the Prodigal Son.
186. The Dog Cart.
187. The Bathers.
188. The Man sitting on the ground.
189. The Woman sitting before a Dutch Stove.
190. A Naked Woman.
191. A Woman preparing to dress after bathing.
192. A Woman with her feet in the water, after bathing.
193. A Woman bathing near the foot of a large tree..
194. The Woman with the Arrow.
195. A Woman sleeping, and a Satyr.
196. Another print on the same subject.
197. A Naked Woman seen from behind.

IX. LANDSCAPES.

198. A Landscape, terminating with the sea, and ruins on the shore.
199. A Landscape with a house, and a large tree by it.
200. Six's Bridge.
201. A View of Omval, near Amsterdam.
202. A View of Amsterdam.
203. The Sportsman.
204. The Three Trees.
205. The Peasant carrying the milk pails.
206. A Landscape, lightly etched, and washed with Indian Ink.
207. The Coach Landscape.
208. A Landscape, unique.
209. A Village near a high road, arched.

I

210. A Village with a square tower, arched.
211. A Farm House and barn.
212. The Shepherd.
213. A Landscape, of an irregular form.
214. A Landscape, with a vista.
215. The Landscape with and without the pointed tower.
216. An Arched Landscape, with cattle.
217. A Large Landscape, with a cottage and a Dutch barn.
218. An Arched Landscape, with an obelisk.
219. A Village with a canal.
220. A Landscape, unique.
221. An Orchard, with a barn.
222. A Large Landscape, with a mill sail seen above the cottage.
223. A Grotto with a brook.
224. A Cottage with white pales.
225. Rembrandt's Father's Mill.
226. The Gold Weigher's Field.
227. Two Landscapes of the same size.
228. A Landscape, with a cow drinking.
229. The same as No. 210.
230. The same as No. 239.
231. A Landscape, unique.
232. A Landscape.
233. A Landscape with a great tree in the middle.
234. A Farmhouse surrounded with white pales.
235. A Landscape, unique.
236. Another Landscape, presque-unique.

X. PORTRAITS OF MEN.

237. A Man in an arbour.
238. A Young Man sitting in a chair.
239. An Old Man with a large beard, an unfinished piece.
240. Bust of an Old Man with a long beard.`
241. The Man with the crucifix and chain.
242. An Old Man with a large white beard.

243. Portrait of a Man with short beard.
244. Abraham Vander Linden.
245. An Old Man in a fur cap, divided in the middle.
246. Janus Silvius.
247. An Old Man sitting at a table.
248. A Young Man musing.
249. Manasseh Ben Israel.
250. Doctor Faustus.
251. Cornelius Hanslo, or Anslo.
252. Clement de Jonge.
253. Abraham France, or Franz.
254. Old Haaring, or Haring, the Burgomaster.
255. Young Haaring, or Haring.
256. John Lutma.
257. Asselyn Crabbetje.
258. Ephraim Bonus.
259. Wtenbogardus, or Wytenbogaert, a Dutch Minister.
260. John Cornelius Sylvius.
261. Wtenbogardus, or Wytenbogaert, the Banker.
262. The Little Coppenol.
263. The Great Coppenol.
264. Van Tol, the Advocate.
265. The Burgomaster Six.

XI. Fancy Heads of Men.

266. Three Original Heads.
267. A Young Man in a Mezetin cap.
268. The Bust of an Old Man with a large beard.
269. The Bust of an Old Man, bald-headed, with a long beard.
270. Two Profiles of a bald-headed man.
271. An Old Man with a pointed beard.
272. The Bust of an Old Man, in an oval.
273. An Old Man with a bald head.
274. An Old Man with a beard.
275. Bust of a Bald Old Man, with his mouth open.

276. Bust of an Old Man in a very high fur cap.

277. Bust of a Man, with a beard from ear to ear.

278. The Slave, with a great cap.

279. A Turkish Slave.

280. Bust of a Man, seen in front, in a cap.

281. Bust of a Man, with curling hair, resembling Rembrandt.

282. Profile of a Bald Old Man.

283. Bust of a Man in a fur cap, stooping.

284. Profile of a Bald Man, coarsely etched.

285. Bust of a man, singularly out-mouthed.

286. An Old Man with a large white beard.

287. A Young Man. A half-length.

288. A Man with a broad-brimmed hat and a ruff.

289. Bust of an Old Man with a large beard and fur cap.

290. An Old Man in a rich velvet cap.

291. An Old Man with a square beard.

292. Bust of an Old Man with a very large beard.

293. A Portrait resembling Rembrandt in a Mezetin cap.

294. A Full Face, laughing.

295. Profile of a Man with a short thick beard.

296. A Philosopher with an hour glass.

297. The Head with the mutilated cap.

298. A Man with moustaches, in a high cap, sitting.

299. Bust of a Man in a cap, one of Rembrandt's first performances.

300. The Man's Head with the cap and stay.

301. Bust of a Man bald-headed.

302. An Old Man sleeping.

303. An Old Man with a very large beard.

304. A grotesque head in a high fur cap.

305. Another grotesque head, with the mouth open.

306. A Man painting.

307. An Old Man's Head.

308. Portrait of an Officer.

309. A Young Man sleeping.

XII. Portraits of Women.

310. The Great Jewish Bride.
311. Saint Catherine.
312. Two Portraits of Old Women.
313. A Young Woman reading.
314. An Old Woman meditating, after reading.
315. Rembrandt's Wife.
316. An Old Woman with her hand on her breast.
317. Rembrandt's Mother.
318. Head of an Old Woman, etched no lower than the chin.
319. Another Head of an Old Woman, etched no lower than the chin.
320. Bust of an Old Woman, lightly etched.
321. An Old Woman in a black veil.
322. A Woman with a basket.
323. A Morisco.
324. Bust of a Woman, the-lower part oval.
325. A Woman in a large hood.
326. An Old Woman's Head.
327. A Woman reading.

XIII. Studies of Heads and other Sketches.

328. The Head of Rembrandt, and other studies.
329. Part of a Horse, and other sketches.
330. Rembrandt's Wife, and five other heads.
331. A Sheet of Sketches.
332. Three Heads of Women.
333. Three Heads of Women, one asleep.
334. Two Women in separate beds, and other sketches.
335. Rembrandt's Head, and several others.
336. Rembrandt's Head, and others.
337. The Sketch of a Dog.
338. Sketch of a Tree, and other subjects.
339. Two Small Figures.
340. Three Profiles of Old Men.

A SUPPLEMENT TO THE CATALOGUE OF THE WORKS OF REMBRANDT.

TRANSLATED FROM THE FRENCH OF PIERRE YVER.

I. PORTRAITS OF REMBRANDT.

1. A Bust of Rembrandt, whilst young.
2. Another Bust of Rembrandt.

II. SCRIPTURE SUBJECTS FROM THE OLD TESTAMENT.

3. Abraham sending away Hagar and Ishmael.
4. The same subject.

III. SCRIPTURE SUBJECTS FROM THE NEW TESTAMENT.

5. The Holy Family.

IV. FANCY PIECES.

6. An Old Man seen in front.
7. An Astrologer, or Old Man asleep.
8. An Alchymist in his laboratory.

V. BEGGARS.

9. A Beggar sitting in an elbow chair, of which the back is seen.
10. A Beggar seen from behind, with a basket of pedlary on his back.
11. A Peasant standing.

VI. LANDSCAPES.

12. A Beautiful Landscape.
13. A Landscape with a canal.
14. A Cottage with a Dutch barn.

15. A Landscape, of great effect.
16. A Landscape, strongly etched.
17. The Hay Waggon.
18. The Castle.
19. The Bull.

VII. Fancy Heads of Men and Women.

20. An Old Man with a short beard.
21. Bust of a Young Man, in an octagon.
22. Bust of a Young Man, lightly sketched.
23. Bust of a Young Man in a Mezetin cap and feather.
24. Bust of a Man.
25. Bust of an Old Man with an aquiline nose.
26. Bust of an Old Man, seen nearly in profile.
27. Bust of a Man in a Ruff, with feathers in his cap.
28. Head of a Man seen in front, in an octagon.
29. Bust of an Old Man with a white beard.
30. Portrait of Titus, Son of Rembrandt.
31. An Old Woman reading.
32. Head of a Woman.   A Study.

INVENTORY OF THE EFFECTS OF REMBRANDT.

Reprinted (with permission) from Smith's " Catalogue Raisonné."

PICTURES, ETC.

IN THE ENTRANCE HALL.

ICTURE, representing the Gingerbread Baker, by *Brauwer.*

A Picture, The Gamblers, by *Brauwer.*

A Picture, a Woman and Child, by *Rembrandt.*

A Picture, the Interior of an Artist's Painting Room, by *Brauwer.*

A Picture, the Interior of a Kitchen, by *Brauwer.*

A Statue of a Woman, in plaster.

Two Children, in plaster.

A Sleeping Child, in plaster.

A Landscape, by *Rembrandt.*

A Landscape, by *Rembrandt.*

A Woman represented standing, by *Rembrandt.*

A Christmas Night Piece, by *Jean Lievensz.*

St. Jerome, by *Rembrandt.*

Dead Hares, a small picture, by *Rembrandt.*

A small picture of a Pig, by *Rembrandt.*

A small Landscape, by *Hercules Segers.*

A Landscape, by *Jean Lievensz.*

A Landscape, by *Jean Lievensz.*

A Landscape, by *Rembrandt.*

A Combat of Lions, by *Rembrandt.*

A Landscape, by moonlight, by *Jean Lievensz.*

A Head, by *Rembrandt.*

A Head, by *Rembrandt.*

A picture of Still Life, objects retouched, by *Rembrandt.*

A Soldier, clad in armour, by *Rembrandt.*

A Skull, and other objects, styled a Vanitas, retouched, by *Rembrandt.*

A Skull, and other objects, styled a Vanitas, retouched, by *Rembrandt.*

A Sea Piece, by *Hendrick Antonisz.*

Four Spanish Chairs, covered with leather.

Two Spanish Chairs, covered in black.

A Plank of Wood.

In the Front Parlour.

A small picture of the Samaritan, retouched, by *Rembrandt.*

The Rich Man, by *Palma Vecchio.*

      (The half of this picture belongs to *Peter de la Tombe.*)

A View of the Back of a House, by *Rembrandt.*

Two Sporting Dogs, done after nature, by *Rembrandt.*

The Descent from the Cross, a large picture, in a gilt frame, by *Rembrandt.*

The Raising of Lazarus, by *Rembrandt.*

A Courtesan Dressing, by *Rembrandt.*

A Woody Scene, by *Hercules Segers.*

Tobias, &c. by *Lastman.*

The Raising of Lazarus, by *Jean Lievensz.*

A Landscape, representing a mountainous country, by *Rembrandt.*

A small Landscape, by *Govert Jansz.*

Two Heads, by *Rembrandt.*

A Picture, *en grisaille*, by *Jean Lievensz.*

A Picture, *en grisaille*, by *Parcelles.*

A Head, by *Rembrandt.*

A Head, by *Brauwer.*

A View on the Dutch Coast, by *Parcelles.*

A View of the same, smaller, by *Parcelles.*

A Hermit, by *Jean Lievensz.*

Two small Heads, by *Lucas Van Valkenburg.*

A Camp on Fire, by the elder *Bassan.*

A Quack Doctor, after *Brauwer.*

Two Heads, by *Jan Pinas.*

A perspective View, by *Lucas Van Leyden.*

A Priest, by *Jean Lievensz.*

A Model, by *Rembrandt.*

A Flock of Sheep, by *Rembrandt.*

A Drawing, by *Rembrandt.*

The Flagellation of Our Lord, by *Rembrandt.*

A Picture, done *en grisaille*, by *Parcelles.*

A Picture, done *en grisaille*, by *Simon de Vlieger.*

A small Landscape, by *Rembrandt.*

A Head of a Woman, after nature, by *Rembrandt.*

A Head, by *Rafaelle Urbino.*

A View of Buildings, after nature, by *Rembrandt.*

A Landscape, after nature, by *Rembrandt.*

A View of Buildings, by *Hercules Segers.*

The Goddess Juno, by *Jacob Pinas.*

A Looking Glass, in a black ebony frame.

An ebony Frame.

A Wine Cooler, in marble.

A Table of walnut tree, covered with a carpet.

Seven Spanish Chairs, with green velvet cushions.

BACK PARLOUR.

A Picture, by *Pietro Testa.*

A Woman with a Child, by *Rembrandt.*

Christ on the Cross, a model, by *Rembrandt.*

A Naked Woman, by *Rembrandt.*

A Copy after a picture, by *Annibal Caracci.*

Two Half Figures, by *Brauwer.*

A Copy, after a picture, by *Annibal Caracci.*

A Sea View, by *Parcelles.*

The Head of an Old Woman, by *Van Dyck.*

A Portrait of a deceased person, by *Abraham Vink.*

The Resurrection, by *A. Van Leyden.*

A Sketch, by *Rembrandt*.

Two Heads, after nature, by *Rembrandt*.

The Consecration of Solomon's Temple, done *en grisaille*, by *Rembrandt*.

The Circumcision, a copy, after *Rembrandt*.

Two small Landscapes, by *Hercules Segers*.

A gilt Frame.

A small oak Table.

Four Shades, for engraving.

A Clothes Press.

Four old Chairs.

Four green Chair Cushions.

A copper Kettle.

A Portmanteau.

THE SALOON.

A Woody Scene, by an *unknown Master*.

An Old Man's Head, by *Rembrandt*.

A large Landscape, by *Hercules Segers*.

A Portrait of a Woman, by *Rembrandt*.

An Allegory of the Union of the Country, by *Rembrandt*.

    (This is probably the picture now in the Collection of Samuel Rogers, Esq.)

A View in a Village, by *Govert Jansz*.

A Young Ox, after nature, by *Rembrandt*.

The Samaritan Woman, a large picture, attributed to *Giorgione*, the half of which

    belongs to *Peter de la Tombe*.

Three antique Statues.

A Sketch of the Entombment, by *Rembrandt*.

The Incredulity of St. Peter, by *Aertje Van Leyden*.

The Resurrection of our Lord, by *Rembrandt*.

The Virgin Mary, by *Rafaelle Urbino*.

A Head of Christ, by *Rembrandt*.

A Winter Scene, by *Grimaer*.

The Crucifixion, by *Lely of Novellaene*.

    (Probably intended for *Novellari*.)

A Head of Christ, by *Rembrandt.*
A Young Bull or Ox, by *Lastman.*
A Vanitas, retouched, by *Rembrandt.*
An Ecce Homo, *en grisaille,* by *Rembrandt.*
Abraham Offering up his Son, by *Jean Lievensz.*
A Vanitas, retouched, by *Rembrandt.*
A Landscape, *en grisaille,* by *Hercules Segers.*
An Evening Scene, by *Rembrandt.*

A large Looking Glass.
Six Chairs, with blue cushions.
An oak Table.
A Table Cloth.
A Napkin Press.
A Wardrobe, or Armoir.
A Bed, and a Bolster.
Two Pillows.
Two Coverlids.
Blue Hangings of a bed.
A Chair.
A Stove.

IN THE CABINET OF ARTS.

A pair of Globes.
A Box containing minerals.
A small Architectural Column.
A Tin Pot.
The Figure of an Infant.
Two pieces of Indian Jadd.
A Japan or Chinese Cup.
A Bust of an Empress.
An Indian Powder Box.
A Bust of the Emperor Augustus.
An Indian Cup.
A Bust of the Emperor Tiberius.

An Indian Work Box, for a lady.

A Bust of Caius.

A pair of Roman Leggings.

Two porcelain Figures.

A Bust of Heraclitus.

Two porcelain Figures.

A Bust of Nero.

Two Iron Helmets.

An Indian Helmet.

An ancient Helmet.

A Bust of a Roman Emperor.

A Negro, cast from nature.

A Bust of Socrates.

A Bust of Homer.

A Bust of Aristotle.

An Antique Head ; done in brown.

A Faustina.

A Coat of Armour, and a Helmet.

A Bust of the Emperor Galba.

A Bust of the Emperor Otho.

A Bust of the Emperor Vitellius.

A Bust of the Emperor Vespasian.

A Bust of the Emperor Titus Vespasian.

A Bust of the Emperor Domitian.

A Bust of Silius Brutus.

Forty-seven specimens of Botany.

Twenty-three specimens of Land and Marine Animals.

A Hammock and two Calabashes.

Eight various objects, in plaster, done from nature.

ON THE LAST SHELF.

A quantity of Shells, Marine Plants, and sundry curious objects, in plaster, done from nature.

An Antique Statue of Cupid.

A small Fuzil, and a Pistol.

A steel Shield, richly embossed with Figures, by Quintin Matsys; very curious and
    rare.

An Antique Powder-horn.

An Antique Powder-horn; Turkish.

A Box, containing Medals.

A Shield of curious workmanship.

Two Naked Figures.

A Cast from the face of Prince Maurice, taken after his death.

A Lion and a Bull, in plaster, after nature.

A number of Walking Sticks.

A long Bow.

BOOKS ON ART.

A Book, containing Sketches, by *Rembrandt.*

A Book, containing Prints, engraved in wood, by *Lucas Van Leyden.*

A Book, containing Prints, engraved in wood, by *Wael and others.*

A Book, containing Etchings, by *Baroccio and Vanni.*

A Book, containing Prints, after *Rafaelle Urbino.*

A gilt Model of a French Bed, by *Verhulst.*

A Book full of Engravings, many of which are double impressions, by *Lucas Van
    Leyden.*

A Book, containing a great number of Drawings, by the best Masters.

A Book, containing a number of fine Drawings, by *Andrea Mantegna.*

A Book, containing Drawings by various masters, and some Prints.

A Book, larger, full of Drawings and Prints.

A Book, containing a number of Miniatures, Wood-cuts, and Copper-plate Prints of the
    various costumes of countries.

A Book full of Prints, by *Old Breughel.*

A Book, containing Prints, after *Rafaello Urbino.*

A Book, containing valuable Prints, by *Rafaelle Urbino.*

A Book, full of Prints, by *Tempesta.*

A Book, containing Wood-cuts and Engravings by *Lucas Cranach.*

A Book, containing Prints, after the *Caracci* and *Guido,* and *Spagnoletti.*

A Book, containing Engravings and Etchings, by *Tempesta.*

A large Folio of Engravings and Etchings, by *Tempesta.*

A large Folio of Engravings and Etchings, various.

A Book, containing Prints, by *Goltius* and *Müller.*

A Book, containing Prints after, *Rafaelle Urbino,* very fine impressions.

A Book, containing Drawings, by *Brauwer.*

A Folio, containing a great number of Prints, after *Titian.*

A number of curious Jars and Venetian Glasses.

An old Book, containing a number of Sketches, by *Rembrandt.*

An old Book, containing a number of Sketches, by *Rembrandt.*

A large Folio of Sketches, by *Rembrandt.*

An empty Folio.

A Backgammon Board.

An antique Chair.

A Book containing Chinese Drawings in miniature.

A large Cluster of White Coral.

A Book full of Prints of Statues.

A Book full of Prints, a complete work, by *Heemskirk.*

A Book full of Sketches, by *Rubens, Van Dyck,* and other Masters.

A Book, containing the Works of *Michael Angelo Buonarotti.*

Two Small Baskets.

A Book, containing Prints of free Subjects, after *Rafaelle, Roest, Annibal, Caracci,* and
　　Giulio Romano.

A Book full of Landscapes, by the most distinguished Masters.

A Book, containing Views of Buildings in Turkey, by *Melchoir Lowick, Hendrick Van
　　Helst,* and others; and also the Costumes of that Country.

An Indian Basket, containing various Engravings, by *Rembrandt, Hollar, Cocq,* and
　　others.

A Book, bound in black leather, containing a selection of Etchings, by *Rembrandt.*

A paper Box, full of Prints, by *Hupe Martin, Holbein, Hans Broemer,* and *Israel Mentz.*

A Book, containing a complete set of Etchings, by *Rembrandt.*

A Folio, containing Academical Drawings of Men and Women, by *Rembrandt.*

A Book, containing Drawings of celebrated Buildings in Rome, and other Views, by the
　　best Masters.

A Chinese Basket, full of various Ornaments.

A Folio.

A Folio.

A Folio, containing Landscapes after Nature, by *Rembrandt.*

A Book, containing a selection of Proof Prints, after *Rubens* and *Jacques Jordaens.*

A Book, full of Drawings, by *Miervelt, Titian,* and others.

A Chinese Basket.

A Chinese Basket, containing Prints of Architectural Subjects.

A Chinese Basket, containing Drawings of various Animals from Nature, by *Rembrandt.*

A Chinese Basket, full of Prints, after *Frans Floris, Buitwael, Goltius,* and *Abraham Bloemart.*

A quantity of Drawings from the Antique, by *Rembrandt.*

Five Books, in quarto, containing Drawings, by *Rembrandt.*

A Book full of Prints of Architectural Views.

The Medea, a Tragedy, by *Jan Six.*

A quantity of Prints, by *Jacques Callot.*

A Book, bound in parchment, containing Drawings of Landscapes, after Nature, by *Rembrandt.*

A Book full of Sketches of Figures, by *Rembrandt.*

A Book full of Sketches, various.

A small Box, with wood divisions.

A Book, containing Views drawn by *Rembrandt.*

A Book, containing fine Sketches.

A Book, containing Statues, after Nature, by *Rembrandt.*

A Book, containing Statues, after Nature, various.

A Book, containing Pen Sketches, by *Peter Lastman.*

A Book, containing Drawings in Red Chalk, by *Peter Lastman.*

A Book, containing Sketches drawn with the Pen, by *Rembrandt.*

A Book, containing Sketches drawn with the Pen, various.

A Book, containing Sketches drawn with the Pen, various.

A Book, containing Sketches drawn with the Pen, various.

A Book, containing Sketches drawn with the Pen, various.

A Book, containing Sketches drawn with the Pen, various.

A Folio of large Drawings of Views in the Tyrol, by *Roeland Savery.*

A Folio full of Drawings by celebrated Masters.

A Book, in quarto, containing Sketches by *Rembrandt.*

A Book of Wood-cuts of the proportions of the Human Figure, by *Albert Durer.*

A Book, containing Engravings by *Jean Lievensz* and *Ferdinand Bol.*

Several parcels of Sketches, by *Rembrandt* and others.

A quantity of Paper of a large size.

A Box, containing Prints by *Van Vliet*, after Pictures by *Rembrandt*.

A Screen, covered with cloth.

A steel Gorget.

A Drawer, containing a Bird of Paradise, and six Forms of divers patterns.

A German Book, containing Prints of Warriors.

A German Book, with Wood-cuts.

Flavius Josephus, in German, illustrated with Engravings, by *Tobias Kinderman*.

An ancient Bible.

A marble Inkstand.

A Cast, in plaster, of Prince Maurice.

IN AN ANTI-CHAMBER OF THE ROOM OF ARTS.

St. Joseph, by *Aertje Van Leyden*.

Three Prints, in frames.

The Salutation.

A Landscape after Nature, by *Rembrandt*.

A Landscape, by *Hercules Segers*.

The Descent from the Cross, by *Rembrandt*.

A Head after Nature.

A Skull, retouched by *Rembrandt*.

A Model, in plaster, of the Bath of Diana, by *Adam Van Vianen*.

A Model from Nature, by *Rembrandt*.

A Picture of Three Puppies, after Nature, by *Titus Van Ryn*.

A Picture of a Book, by *Titus Van Ryn*.

A Head of the Virgin, by *Titus Van Ryn*.

The Flagellation, a copy after *Rembrandt*.

A Landscape, by Moonlight, retouched by *Rembrandt*.

A Naked Woman, a Model from Nature, by *Rembrandt*.

An unfinished Landscape from Nature, by *Rembrandt*.

A Horse painted from Nature, by *Rembrandt*.

A small Picture, by *Young Hals*.

A Fish, after Nature.

A Model, in plaster, of a Bason, adorned with Figures, by *Adam Van Vianen*.

An old Chest.

L

Four Chairs, with black leather seats.
A Table.

Thirty-three pieces of Armour, and Musical Instruments.
Sixty pieces of Indian Armour, and several Bows, Arrows, and Darts.
Thirteen bamboo Pipes, and several Flutes.
Thirteen Objects, consisting of Bows, Arrows, Shields, &c.
A number of Heads and Hands, moulded from Nature, together with a Harp, and a
    Turkish Bow.
Seventeen Hands and Arms, moulded from Nature.
Some Stag Horns.
Five ancient Casques.
Four Long Bows, and Cross Bows.
Nine Gourds and Bottles.
Two modelled Busts of Bartholt Been and his Wife.
A plaster Cast from a Grecian Antique.
A Bust of the Emperor Agrippa.
A Bust of the Emperor Aurelius.
A Head of Christ, of the size of life.
A Head of a Satyr.
A Sibyl—antique.
The Laocoon—antique.
A large Marine Vegetable.
A Vitellius.
A Seneca.
Three or four Antique Heads of Women.
A metal Cannon.
A quantity of Fragments of Antique Dresses of divers colours.
Seven Musical stringed Instruments.
Two small Pictures, by *Rembrandt.*

Twenty Objects, consisting of Halberds and Swords of various kinds.
Dresses of an Indian Man and Woman.

Five Cuirasses.

A wooden Trumpet.

A picture of Two Negroes, by *Rembrandt.*

A Child, by *Michael Angelo Buonarotti.*

IN THE SHED.

The skins of a Lion and a Lioness, and two Birds.

A large Piece representing Diana.

A Bittern, done from Nature, by *Rembrandt.*

IN A SMALL ROOM.

Ten Paintings of various sizes, by *Rembrandt.*

A Bed.

IN THE KITCHEN.

A pewter Pot.

Several Pots and Pans.

A small Table.

A Cupboard.

Several old Chairs.

Two Chair Cushions.

IN THE PASSAGE.

Nine Plates.

Two earthen Dishes.

THE LINEN (THEN AT THE WASHERWOMAN'S).

Three Shirts.

Six Pocket Handkerchiefs.

Twelve Napkins.

Three Table Cloths.

Some Collars, and Wristbands.

The preceding Inventory was made on the 25th and 26th of July, 1656.

CHISWICK PRESS :—PRINTED BY WHITTINGHAM AND WILKINS,
TOOKS COURT, CHANCERY LANE.